The Family Cannon

The Family Cannon

Stories
By
Halina Duraj

Augury
BOOKS

Augury Books
New York, New York

For Hallie —
who's a dedicated
aunt! Thank
you for coming!!
Love,
Halin
5/10/14

Published in the United States of America
First Edition

Cover Image by Dave Bledsoe, FreeVerse Photography
Book Design by Daniel Estrella
ISBN: 978-0-9887355-3-8

For reproduction inquiries or other information,
please visit www.augurybooks.com.

Acknowledgments

Thanks to the editors of the journals in which these stories originally appeared:

"American Cousin." *Descant*, Fall 2007.

"George Foreman Grill, George Foreman Grill." *The Ocean State Review*, Issue 2.1, 2012.

"Groceries" (now "Oysters"). *Grain*, Volume 34, Number 1, Summer 2006.

"In Kudova" (now "In Kudowa"). *Confrontation*, Number 98/99, Spring/Summer 2007.

"Tenants." *Third Coast*, Spring 2008.

"The Company She Keeps." *Hayden's Ferry Review*, Spring 2010.

"The Family Cannon." *Fiction*, Number 55.

"The Painting on Florianska Street" (now "The Painting"). *Porcupine*, Volume 8, Issue 1, 2004.

"Witness." *PRISM International*, Volume 44, Number 1, Fall 2005.

Thanks also to Kate Angus and Kimberly Steele at Augury Books for selecting this book and editing it with such care. I am so grateful to my teachers: Kirk Colvin, Pam Houston, Lynn Freed, Francois Camoin, and especially Melanie Rae Thon. Thank you to friends in the writing communities at U.C. Davis and the University of Utah for help with early drafts of these stories. Special thanks to Jacob Paul for the cannon, and enormous thanks to friends who read the manuscript in its entirety: Katie Farris, Adam Veal, Christine Marshall, and Esther Lee. And finally, thanks to Laurel Doud and Claudia Parker for early and continuing encouragement; Ann Milner, Randi Mills, Mark Burry, Jen Beschorner, and Shannon Gullett, for friendship; and my family, for everything.

Stories

The Family Cannon

I was the only kid I knew whose father had an alias. The utility bills came to our house addressed to Zbigniew Zaszewski, but my father's name was Witek Witecki. When I asked him about it, he said he bought our house in California a long time ago, after he'd escaped the Nazis in Germany. He'd used a different name back then; even though World War II was over, Nazis still hid everywhere. He kept the house under his alias because Nazis could hunt him down and kill him, even in a town as pretty and peaceful as ours.

This news led to a lot of restless nights for me. Every night my father came to check that the windows of my first-floor bedroom were locked; I would lie awake long after. But by the fall of 1989, when I started high school, I thought less about the Nazis. Then my father announced that a Nazi had moved in next door.

I asked how he knew he was a Nazi, and my father said he had a German last name. That's how you could tell, he said. Wouldn't he take a different name, too, I asked? They don't need to, my father said. They're not afraid of anyone.

The new neighbor did have a German last name—Wahler— but otherwise he seemed pretty un-Nazi-like to me. He was a balding bachelor architect who lined his front yard with rows and rows of terracotta flowerpots. In the first few weeks after he'd arrived, he exchanged pleasantries with my mother about the merits of annuals versus perennials, and he smiled at me when I passed his house on my way home from orchestra practice with Eddie O'Connor. Overall, Mr. Wahler seemed nothing like what I imagined a Nazi to be.

Sometime around late September, Mr. Wahler tore down the fence between his house and ours and put up a beautiful wall: five feet high, half a foot thick, and plastered in ecru stucco. The only problem with the wall was that it overlapped our property by two inches, or so my father believed. He said he knew every inch of the goddamn quarter acre he'd worked eight hours a day to pay off for twenty-some years and he knew when a goddamn Nazi had taken two inches. He'd know even when a Nazi took half an inch, he said.

So one Saturday in September, while my mother and I dug dandelions out of the front lawn, my father went next door and told Mr. Wahler that he better knock down his goddamn Nazi wall and rebuild it on his own goddamn Nazi property. Mr. Wahler laughed, then understood my father was serious.

"Of course not," Mr. Wahler said. He seemed a little bewildered.

Then my father leaned in and grabbed the doorknob and slammed the door in his own face. I think he must have momentarily forgotten that he had been the one to go over there, or he thought that slamming the door on himself also slammed it on Mr. Wahler. Or maybe it was a sign of what was going to happen to my father's mind in the end. I've never been sure.

My father always started his Nazi story with the words, "The night Hitler came for me...." For a long time, I failed to understand how Hitler could have single-handedly rounded up all six million Jews and the non-Jewish Poles like my father who were used for slave labor. Until I reached a certain age, I assumed Hitler must have had some kind of magic sleigh.

My father was sixteen the night Hitler came for him in October of 1940. The SS-men's truck rolled right up into my grandmother's barnyard in Poland at four in the morning. Soldiers dragged my father at gunpoint out of the bed he shared with two of his brothers. He was the only child arrested; his brothers all had papers. He was the youngest and his only job had been to help his widowed mother on their farm.

He spent four years getting trundled between four different slave labor camps, the last and worst of which was Auschwitz. One night he and some other inmates took a chance: During a march back to camp through the woods in which they'd been digging ditches, my father broke from the line and ran. He evaded bullets. Nighttime and a tree saved his life. The ground-sweeping branches of a fir kept him hidden from the SS-men's flashlights. There were no dogs.

"If there had been dogs," my father always said, "I wouldn't be here to tell you this." The SS-men fired a few shots into the trees and gave up. My father spent the night under the branches, motionless. Then he crept out of the woods, crawled beneath a train, and clung to its underbelly for the fifteen-hour ride into Czechoslovakia and freedom.

After the war was over, he stole a bike and made his way home to Poland. It took months. He rode the bike right up to the barn, where his mother was milking the cows. She had thought he was dead. She overturned the milk can and splashed through milk all around her ankles. She threw her arms around his body—bones, nothing but bones, was what she said.

My father was especially fond of getting down on the kitchen floor to reenact the entire escape—especially for dinner guests or drop-in visitors. He sprawled on the linoleum beneath invisible tree branches. He always played both parts. He narrated in Polish but shouted and yelled in German. He stomped his feet—SS boots. And then, suddenly, he'd be the trembling boy again, lying under a fir tree. Our guests fidgeted, glanced at the clock; my mother whispered apologies.

After the kitchen-floor reenactments, our guests went home, and my father entered a kind of a trance from which he did not emerge for hours. On those nights, his dreams woke the house.

I knew that my father had had a hard, hard life, and mine was so much easier by comparison that I couldn't ever dare complain about anything. But I was thirteen, and all I could think about were the things I didn't have, like more than one friend (more than one made your grades drop). And I wanted but didn't have the hundred-dollar designer jeans that all the girls were wearing. And I wanted—more than anything—permission to go to the Christmas dance with a boy I liked. A boy, say, like Eddie O'Connor. One date. But boys were never discussed. Boys were implausible.

***

In October, my birthday month, my father cut down my favorite tree—the feathery pepper between my bedroom and Mr. Wahler's wall. He didn't cut it all the way down. He amputated it, leaving behind a forked trunk that protruded four feet above the fence, in the direct line of sight of Mr. Wahler's dining room windows.

My imaginary friends had once inhabited those mysterious, veiled branches. With the tree gone, I kept my shades drawn all the time. They were the white vinyl kind, with the little cords you pulled on slightly, drawing them down a tiny bit first before they'd snap up all on their own. My mother put them up in the morning. I waited until my father came home from work before I yanked them back down. Either he didn't hear or didn't care. Mr. Wahler kept his shades down, too.

Then my father bought a used camper, a Week N Der with orange and brown stripes. He unloaded it into the space between our house and Mr. Wahler's wall, onto a platform he'd built from cinder blocks and two-by-fours. The platform raised the Week N Der into Mr. Wahler's view, alongside the forked stump.

When the Week N Der didn't do the trick, my father made some minor adjustments. He piled our old doghouse on top, garbage bags weighed down with lawn and hedge trimmings, more cinder blocks, a rusted bike frame, our old push-mower. Mr. Wahler installed classy wooden shutters from the inside—the kind that you adjusted with the turn of a wand to tilt the blinds and let in the light but keep out the view. Sometimes thin strips of light shone around the edges of the windows, and muffled laughter drifted across our yard. Those nights, cars I didn't recognize parked tightly along Mr. Wahler's curb and in front of our house, too. My father wrote notes that said, *Friends of Nazis not allowed to park here*, and slipped the notes under the windshield wipers.

Next came the sign. The sign was a whitewashed sheet of plywood, three-by-four feet, nailed to a fifteen-foot two-by-four and driven deep into the lawn. In giant black letters, my father carefully stenciled, WAHLER MOVE YOUR WALL.

My father posted it in the front yard the morning of my birthday, as if it were a special present to me and to every kid who passed our house on the way to the high school. I stood outside and looked at it. My father climbed into his truck and started the engine. My mother in her bathrobe handed him his lunch bag and thermos through the rolled-down window.

"*Wesołe Imieniny*, Magda," my father yelled. Happy Birthday. He smiled and waved. Pounding in the sign had put him in a good mood.

I had long ago explained my father—what I understood of him—to my one friend, Clara, who said her mother was crazy, too, though not in the same way.

"Wow," Clara said when she saw the sign in the yard. "That's different."

My father had told me I shouldn't have picked Clara as my one friend because her parents were separated. Still, Clara and I were allowed to participate in approved activities together, like biking to the library. To neutralize the influence of Clara's fractured American family, my father stressed frequently the importance of meeting and marrying a Polish man someday. He was saving up to send me to Poland after I graduated from college. If at that time I wanted to meet a nice Polish engineer and bring him home to start a family, I'd have my father's blessing.

In the meantime, all I could do with Eddie O'Connor was walk home from orchestra practice. He lived two houses down from me, in one of the big new peach-colored mini-mansions that had started being built a year or two before. From the front, it seemed to fill its whole lot, fence to fence. In back, there was a pool and a pool-house and a hot tub. Eddie's father was the vice-president of Brite Fresh Toothpaste, and Eddie had the most beautiful teeth of anyone I'd ever met: square and white and even.

Eddie and I both played the violin in orchestra, although he was first chair and I was second. I had to play because my father wanted to be reminded of the boy in the bunk beneath his in Auschwitz who had played the fiddle late at night, very softly and mournfully. Eddie played because he'd been given a violin when he was three and had shown an immediate flair.

He was so good that he already had a spot reserved at Juilliard, and all the students knew he only played with our mediocre and mostly-out-of-tune high school orchestra because our conductor was a childhood friend of Eddie's dad and had begged Eddie's parents to let him play. Eddie didn't even go to our high school— he got homeschooled by a different Stanford grad student in every subject. Eddie said he liked our orchestra and needed the extra practice, but he was just being polite.

When we walked home together on Mondays, I made sure I wasn't walking on whatever side he swung his violin so I wouldn't accidentally bump it. It was an eighty-thousand-dollar, two-hundred-year-old Guarnerius—one notch below a Stradivarius, he confessed once, a red flush to his cheeks. "It's really more of an investment," he said. "For my parents."

My parents didn't have investments, unless you consider a mail-order, life-size replica Civil War cannon an investment. It must have arrived while we were at orchestra practice that first Monday of November, because it hadn't been there when I came home for a snack after school, and it was so very there when Eddie and I got to my house after practice. My parents were lugging it into place in the center of the front lawn, positioning it beneath the Wahler-Move-Your-Wall sign.

There it was, dark and shiny and undeniably cannon-like, an iron barrel flanked by two spoked wheels, pointing straight at the wall and bungalow next door.

"Well, looks like we got a cannon," I said. I didn't look at Eddie.

"Looks like you did," Eddie said.

There wasn't much you could say after that, so I said, "See you later," and turned up the drive. I figured that was pretty much it for my friendship—or anything else—with Eddie O'Connor.

But Eddie called out, "Hey." I turned around. He had started walking backwards, slowly. "Nice playing today," he said, and smiled.

He must have felt sorry for me just then, because there was rarely anything nice about my playing. And if Eddie O'Connor was feeling sorry for me, I was going to feel sorry for myself, too.

I moped all through dinner and homework and all the way up until I opened my violin case to practice. I took out my bow and tightened it, then lifted the lid of the rosin pocket. A little origami frog made of notebook paper sat inside. My bow clattered to the ground. I unfolded the paper so fast I almost ripped it. I read, *Would you go to the Christmas dance with me?* There was a little cartoon drawing of a frog, beside which was scrawled, *Eddie*.

I asked my father if I could go to the dance. "Eddie plays the violin," I said.

My father laughed, which seemed like a bad sign. If the idea of me going to the dance with a boy could seem only funny and not at all threatening, it was in no way in the realm of the possible.

The next evening, my father called me over to the kitchen table. He had propped his feet up on another chair. He picked at his teeth with a toothpick.

"Sit down," he said, motioning with his toothpick toward the chair where his feet were. I perched on the edge. "So. This boy. He plays the violin? What is his last name?"

"O'Connor," I said.

My father nodded. "The Irish," he said. "They've had a hard time." He emphasized "hard time" with two jabs of his toothpick in the air. "Almost as bad as us," he said.

He put the toothpick back in his mouth. "What does his father do?"

"He makes toothbrushes." I justified the lie with the fact that my father always said he made missiles, but what he meant—what my mother later clarified—was that he made parts for machines that made missiles.

My father nodded. He continued picking at his teeth. The refrigerator thrummed, then clicked off. My mother ran water in the laundry room sink. And then something miraculous happened. Maybe my father felt an overwhelming camaraderie with the entire Irish nation, or maybe it was the image of a tired Irishman working in a toothbrush factory. Most likely, it was the buoyant mood he was in because he now had a cannon. Whatever the cause, he said, "*Ja*, Magda, good. It's okay. Go to this dance."

Go to this dance. Go to this dance.

I walked out of the kitchen, stunned, dazed. I passed my mother in the laundry room. She was wringing the water out of my father's extra-strength support socks. He only had two pairs, so she washed them every other night.

"Quick, go practice," she whispered. "Nicely!"

That night, I tugged softly on the window-shade tassel and guided it up. I could make out the specter of the tree stump but I didn't care because I could also see stars, which were the same stars Eddie could have seen from his room right then, if he had been looking outside and thinking of me, thinking of him.

My luck seemed impossibly good, and the Christmas dance seemed impossibly far away. I told myself that even if my father changed his mind, I would have known what it was like to be a normal girl, going to a normal dance, with a normal, beautiful boy.

I left the window shade up so I could fall asleep to starlight.

I wanted to blame Mr. Wahler for what happened the following Sunday, but I couldn't. It really wasn't his fault. None of it was. Obviously, he was feeling a little threatened by the cannon—not because it was a real weapon—it wasn't, of course—but because it hinted at the existence of real weapons. And so he had every right to poke his head over the top of the wall that Sunday morning to say that he took the cannon a little personally. That the sign had been bad, and the tree and the camper had been bad, but the cannon was a physical threat and he felt compelled to notify the authorities, or at least call a lawyer.

My father went to the garden shed—the same garden shed in which I'd been storing my soccer balls and volleyball net and Trac-Ball mitts and baseball bat, even though my father thought baseball was the most insipid American sport. That morning he didn't seem to mind baseball so much. He didn't reach for a Trac-Ball mitt. He took the bat and held it low as he marched back to the fence.

When Mr. Wahler looked up, my father cracked him on the side of the neck and watched him crumple out of sight.

When it was clear that the sirens were stopping outside of our house, the neighbors came out in pajamas and bathrobes. I would have been curious, too. Especially if it was the house with the sign and the camper and the cannon.

Policemen handcuffed my father and put him in the back of a police car. The entire neighborhood watched but pretended not to. The entire neighborhood poked their fading flowerbeds and raked their lawns. My mother said I still had to bike to church. I rode down the driveway and past the neighbors who lingered in small groups and pairs.

"Pray for him," my mother had urged. I forgot to ask if she meant my father or Mr. Wahler, so I prayed for them both—a little halfheartedly for my father. And because I'd seen Eddie O'Connor's dad—though not, thankfully, Eddie—in a maroon, velour jogging suit standing across from our house with their golden retriever, I prayed for myself, too.

My father spent all that day and night in jail. The next morning, I'd already begun walking to school when a low-slung sedan pulled up outside the house. I looked over my shoulder. My father got out, waved at the driver, and said something to him in what sounded like Spanish. I kept walking, as if that were not my father and not my house. That night, I learned that my father had gotten a ride home with the family of a Mexican man he'd befriended in the holding cell.

I tried to hold my head high all day at school. I was only sure that Eddie's dad had seen the incident, and since Eddie didn't come to school until orchestra, no one else could know.

After orchestra practice, when Eddie and I were walking home, he very shyly and awkwardly told me his dad didn't want him to go the dance with me. He said he wasn't scared of my dad, but his dad was, and if it were up to him, he'd still want to take me to the dance. And he blushed and bumped his violin case against the side of his thigh.

I said, "Maybe you shouldn't be doing that," and he said, "Maybe you're right." I stuck out my hand and said, "No big deal," even though it was. I said that if I had seen his father get hauled away in a police car, I wouldn't have wanted to go to the dance with him either. Which was just an out-and-out lie, since his dad would have been booked for some white-collar crime like embezzlement, not assault with intent to maim. Eddie laughed and we shook hands, and my heart thudded because we were touching.

That night I cried into my pillow because his hand had felt so good in mine and I wouldn't get to dance with him ever. My mother sat on my bed and told me that high school was long and maybe Eddie's dad would forget that my dad was crazy, and maybe we could go to a different dance together, maybe even the spring dance. But I never found another note in my rosin pocket, and the following year Juilliard took Eddie as a teen prodigy.

By mid-December, Mr. Wahler had come home from the hospital. He puttered around his pots in the late afternoons, but never without his foam neck brace. My father bought his own neck brace, and wore it mockingly in the yard for a while. He insisted that he'd hardly tapped the man, and the injuries were all a ruse to bankrupt him with hospital bills.

The night of the Christmas dance was also the night my father's new friend from jail and his family came over for dinner. By the end of the meal, my father lay on the kitchen floor, shouting in German and Polish and trembling and stomping his feet.

I couldn't stand to be around my father just then. There he was, on the kitchen floor, escaping the Nazis again and again, and I had to feel sorry for him—I had to. But I didn't want to. Maybe I hadn't endured four years of slave labor and maybe Hitler hadn't come for me in the night, but there was a boy with whom I could have been dancing, touching hands, and it was my father's fault that I wasn't. He didn't care. For once, I wanted my life to stand alone, beyond comparison with monstrous things.

I put on a jacket and sat on the cold bench outside the picture window. I couldn't even call Clara because she was at the dance with Tim McLeider, who wore headgear for his braces and had funny hips for a boy. But still—she was at the dance! I looked at the cannon and waited for my mother to come find me.

"I'm trying really hard not to," I said, "but I hate Dad."

My mother nodded. "So do I sometimes," she said. "It's okay." She put her around me, and it helped somehow to hate him together.

By spring, the court-appointed surveyor said my father had known two inches when he'd seen two inches. A construction crew knocked down the wall at Mr. Wahler's expense and built a new wall.

And then my father was happy for a while.

Sometime while I was away at college, my father's mind began to go—not in the way it had always been gone, but in a new way. My mother said he sometimes drove off in his big gray truck, wearing his blue leather coat and Scottish tweed cap. Occasionally, he traded the tweed cap for my childhood bike helmet—because even with a seat belt you weren't safe—and he drove up and down El Camino Real wearing a yellow helmet too small for his head. He often forgot why he'd left home in the first place and couldn't figure out how to get back. Sometimes he'd make it home by dark. Other times he'd drive around until late at night before finally stopping to ask someone for directions.

On one of my visits from college, my father took me to his big oak desk in the living room, rummaged in the back of a drawer, and pulled out a black-and-white photograph with curled and yellowed edges. It showed a group of men, all with skeletal faces. All of them wore dark, striped uniforms and stood in front of barbed-wire fencing. Some of the men smiled toothless smiles; most stared into the camera with empty, dark-circled eyes.

"Look," my father said. I had never seen the picture before, so I did not know what to look for. Finally, my father pointed to a figure in the back row: a man with close-shorn hair and bones for cheeks. The man in the picture was not smiling.

"This," he said, "was the happiest day of my life." I nodded, but still I did not understand. Then I turned over the photograph and in my father's careful right-angled script were the words, "Auschwitz, Liberation, 1945." I did not know if this was dementia or if this was the truth. I left my father digging around in the back of his desk. I went to my mother and held out the photo.

She told me that the picture was part of the truth. My father had not escaped Auschwitz, like he said again and again. He had been liberated in 1945.

But the kitchen-floor act was also true. He had once lain under a tree all night while soldiers searched for him, and he had gripped the underbelly of a train for fifteen hours into freedom. Except it had been Russian soldiers with flashlights, not Nazis.

After the liberation, yes, my father had stolen the bike. He had ridden home to his mother and she splashed through milk to hold him, yes. Then he was drafted into the Communist army. But army life was too much like the camps, my mother said. Told when to get up, when to march. Only a little more food, that's all.

"Deserting the army is a great disgrace in Poland," she said. "Not something you want your children to know."

It was the kind of news that makes you want to think about things—especially things you've always believed to be true—so I took a tour around the yard I'd grown up in. I looked at the wall, identical to the first but two inches farther away, and Mr. Wahler's shutters, as tightly closed as always. The sign was long gone, and my mother had convinced my father to sell the camper we'd never used for recreational purposes.

Over Mr. Wahler's house, I could see the rose-brown tiles of the O'Connors' roof. I'd heard from my mother that Eddie's dad had died of a heart attack the year before. The cannon, of course, still stood where it had always stood, because once you've installed a cannon, it's not the easiest thing to budge. My mother had done her best to disguise it with flowers and shrubs, and had even rooted a little ivy in a clod of dirt in the mouth.

I climbed onto the cannon and surveyed the yard and the neighborhood and turned around to see the big picture window, behind which my father stood. He wore his coat and helmet.

Perhaps he'd been planning on going for a drive, but instead he came out into the front yard and walked up to me.

"I want to ask you something," he said. "I want to know—what did you think of your childhood? Did you have a good childhood?"

"Well," I said, "it was better than some." He smiled, looked off to the side with his head bent, helmet on for safety, as if listening for something in the distance—thunder, or cicadas. Then he nodded, as if he'd heard what he'd been listening for. He looked back at me.

"Good," he said. "That's all I wanted."

He held out his hand and I shook it. And then he strode toward the driveway, climbed into the truck, and roared off onto—I assumed—one of his aimless missions. As for me, I sat on the cannon a while yet, thinking, but that, too, began to feel aimless. Inside the house somewhere was my mother, making tea or rinsing socks. I climbed down from the cannon and went to find her. It seemed important just then—a luxury, too—to sit with the living.

In Kudowa

One October evening years before I was born, my mother stepped off a curb in Trzebinia, Poland, and was struck by a speeding bakery truck. The force of the truck hurled her twelve feet down the street. And landed her a husband.

And what a catch he was, I tell her, looking up at the ceiling tiles.

She's told me this story a hundred times. I know it by heart, but of late, she's taken to getting this faraway look in her eye, as if she were still in Poland, when the hours drag by my dad's bed. He's not much of a conversationalist anymore (stroke, aphasia), so she's started telling all the old stories again, and she's taken up knitting. Mostly scarves for the homeless, although all the nursing home staff have put in orders. And she's grateful for visitors. Especially me, who doesn't mind her stories—who prefers them, in fact, to questions about my own life.

When I pushed open the heavy door to my father's room this morning, my mother stared at me for a moment, then threw her hands up in the air, laughed, and said, "Magda, I didn't recognize!" And then, excitedly, "You know what that means in Poland, when mother doesn't recognize daughter? Daughter gets married soon!"

She also believes that dropping a fork means a stranger will visit, and roosters bring prosperity.

I say, "I know Mom. You said that last week."

I'm not getting married soon, maybe not ever. I won't even live with Sam, my boyfriend. I'm not old-fashioned. I just like having my own apartment. I like my stuff and I don't want to see anyone else's stuff mingled in with it. My mother doesn't understand why Sam and I haven't gotten married yet. We've been together six years. My mother calls him the "sweetest boy in whole world." She tells me I won't find anyone better. Maybe I won't, but what does she know? She wants to knit him a scarf. I tell her Sam doesn't wear scarves.

Each time I visit, she asks me if I've brought any of Sam's clothes to repair. She likes to fix things; it helps pass the time. And she does a good job; in Poland, she was a seamstress. But I don't bring Sam's clothes, even though he's got hardly a shirt that doesn't have a tear in it somewhere, or a missing button. It feels too intimate, too familial, my mother fixing my boyfriend's clothes.

Sam's pathetic with needle and thread, and even though I know how to sew buttons on—when I was five my mother gave me her button box and an old washcloth and told me to sew buttons all around the edge—I let Sam take his stuff to the tailor. I can't remember a night when my mother wasn't darning or hand washing a pair of my father's black, extra-calf-support socks. Or a morning when he didn't charge out of the house to his truck, keys in hand, motioning with one arm to the thermos and lunch bag that sat on the kitchen counter. And without a word, my mother would pick them up, follow him out in her robe, and hand them to him once he had climbed into the truck.

I ruffle through the plastic shopping bag at my mother's feet—full of scarves she's finished: thick, scratchy wool in hunter green, slate blue, burgundy. I go into the adjoining bathroom, drape a blue one over one shoulder, burgundy over the other. I look in the mirror. I can't decide, I say. Her fingers move so fast, the needles click like someone working a ten key.

"Come here," she says. She squints up at me through her thick glasses. The frames are pink, and they fan out from her face. They remind me of butterfly wings, that kind of widening curve at the edge. "They both look good on you," she says.

And then she tells me all the same old stories again—of how they met and what it was like to come to America—as if she's telling me for the first time, as if she's revealing secrets she hadn't wanted me to know before.

"If my head had hit the curb," she says, "Ach, *kapliczka*." That's one of those shrines you see on the side of the road, shrines the family erects at the spot where someone died in a car accident. In Poland, it's usually a statue of the Virgin Mary, or just a cross with a ribbon tied around it.

But my mother's head didn't hit the curb. It hit the flat of the road, and she bounced. Landing, she says, with blood pooling all around her head and her coat flung up around her waist and her skirt hitched to her knees. I don't know how she could know this, seeing as she was unconscious—but this is what she tells me, and, as always, I let her make up the parts she wants. She has proof of the blood, though. A scar zigzags along her hairline. When I was little, I thought she had been struck by lightning, it looked so much like a lightning bolt.

There were no ambulances in Trzebinia then, and when the taxi driver pulled over and saw the blood and the body in the men's arms, he tried to drive off, but the men were already opening the door and shoving her in. She said she must have bled all over his back seat, that she wished she knew who it was who picked her up and forced her into the taxi—she'd liked to have thanked him.

"Maybe you could have married him," I said.

"Magda," she chides. "Watch out, maybe *Tata* hears." She looks over at Dad and shakes her head, but she's smiling. Then she looks down at the crimson loops she's made quicksilver fast on her needles. I look at Dad too. He's asleep, although for him, being asleep isn't all that different from being awake. I'm glad he's asleep. He's got this look in his eyes when they're open, like he's drowning inside himself and it's not any kind of water we know. I look at his close-shorn gray hair, massive nose, his mouth open so I see his dulled gold canine. A giant wooden cross the size of a dinner fork hangs around his neck on a thin satin ribbon. It rests on his hospital gown, just below the permanent-inked name of the nursing home. My mother put the cross around his neck the day he came here.

After the first few weeks in the Trzebinia hospital, her head wound seemed to have healed and she was due to be released, but when she got out of bed and leaned over to pull on her skirt, she heard a bubbling come up her chest and into her throat. When she straightened, she heard the blurb-blurb-blurb go back down. She told the nun who told the doctor who ordered x-rays and then poked a giant syringe through her back (no anesthetic) to pull out vials of red-tinted fluid. After that, she stayed a good while longer.

When she went back to work in March, she was weak, and her supervisor gave her a paid month at Kudowa, a convalescent resort in the countryside. "One good thing about the Communists," my mother says, "they give you health care at least." A nurse and doctor on site at the factory. Paid leave. She glances over at my father. This room in the nursing home costs them $5,000 a month.

Kudowa was the best month of my mother's life. She had nothing to do but go on walks through meadows bursting with April wildflowers, attend morning Mass in the little chapel every day, and chat with other patients. She finished *Anna Karenina* and *Dr. Zhivago* that month and had three meals cooked for her every day. She prayed three times a day, too—for a sign, a miracle. She was twenty-nine, still single, had been a seamstress for nine years. All of her friends were married, had been married since they were twenty, twenty-one. She wanted to be married too. She wanted adventure. I think she expected to find them in the same place.

On her second-to-last day in Kudowa, there was going to be a dance, and she didn't want to go, but some of the other patients convinced her. You'll have a cup of coffee, they said. You'll dance a little. Come on. Why not? So she put on her black silk dress with the white collar and high-heeled black shoes and her strand of pearls that she'd saved a little bit each month to buy, and she curled her hair up into a lovely bouffant and went, mostly against her will.

She leaves things out. For instance, the fact that he had deserted the Polish Army after the liberation. He clung to the underbelly of a train overnight, across the border into Czechoslovakia. Eventually he boarded a ship out of Denmark, bound for Connecticut.

He landed in America with seven dollars in his pocket, peeled potatoes in the ship's galley to help buy his passage. One cold Connecticut winter was enough. After six months on the East Coast, my father bought an old Buick, drove it west until he found that warm, lush state everyone talked about. Once he was an American citizen, he went back to Poland with two missions: get some gold dental work done (cheaper there) and cruise the convalescent homes to find a suitable wife. Someone broken enough to be submissive but still strong enough to work hard. Someone who would give birth to sons and wouldn't want to rearrange the furniture.

At the dance in Kudowa, my father sat down next to a little old widow and looked around. Mom caught his eye. I can see how she must have been sitting, knees together, a little prim, picking up her white porcelain coffee cup and sipping it, smiling softly at something somebody said, sitting round the white tablecloth in the broad gazebo with the Roman columns and the marble steps leading to a sunken dance floor, and the band at one end. Dusk approached the edges of the dance floor, but, within the gazebo, everything was lit up with candles and little strung-up lights.

My father leaned over to the widow and asked "if the lady was acquainted with that lady over there," and she said, "Yes, of course, sir, Pani Julka is a very good woman. The gentleman would do well to get to know her." And then my father said, "Then maybe I'll ask her to dance." And the widow said, "The gentleman should definitely do that."

The widow excused herself, sidled over to where my mother sat, said, "Excuse me, miss, don't look now, but the man sitting over there is from America and has been asking about you." Mom sort of half-smiled (as she does now, telling me this in her modest, who-would-be-looking-at-me way). "I looked around, but I did not know who or what," she tells me. "And I did not bother myself with it."

Dad walked up, and they danced. Mom pinches her mouth together, widens her eyes, and raises her eyebrows as far as they'll go. "He danced so fast—you know *Tata*—one two, one two." She tries to show me, laying the knitting needles in her lap and swinging her arms around briskly, an imitation of a man's arms encircling a woman. "He did not follow the music at all." She was mortified, but all she said was, "If the gentleman would only dance a little slower!"

After they danced, they talked for a while. She told him why she was there, the bakery truck, and he talked about America. And then he said, "Look through your window tomorrow at three and you'll see me in the street. Come down." And the next day at three she looked out her window and saw him, as he'd said, in front of the post office. He was wearing a black wool three-quarter-length coat and a black beret. His hands were thrust deep in his pockets, his shoulders hunched, though it wasn't that cold, and he glanced from side to side.

"Didn't you think that was strange?" I ask. "Wouldn't a normal man have come to your door?"

"It was odd," she admits. But she didn't really care. He had a house in America. Also, she hadn't known then that he'd spent eleven years after the war as a con artist in Berlin alleys. It would have made more sense. They walked together a while and talked some more. He told her about California, where it was sunny all year long. He didn't tell her about Auschwitz. But she knew something was wrong. It was in his eyes. The way he was always looking around, over his shoulder, restless. His face was so skinny, his eyes a little sunken. She did the math. Seventeen years since the liberation, but all of it still hanging around him like a bad smell.

They walked down the single dirt road of the little resort town, out to the white chapel right at the edge of the wildflower fields. She asked him if he'd like to pray with her and he laughed, a little bitterly.

"Go ahead. I'll wait here."

This shook her to the knees. She wouldn't marry a pagan. She was grateful that she was outside a church just when she needed one most. She went inside and kneeled against one of the hard wooden pews. The chapel was lit with two banks of votive candles on either side of the altar. A large icon of the Black Madonna stood on an easel to the right of the altar. The stained glass windows cast colored shapes onto the wood floor. She laid her forehead on her interlaced fingers and prayed for a sign.

One of the old village women, bent and gnarled, dressed all in black with a black scarf over her head, shuffled up the aisle and sat in the pew behind my mother.

"Your husband looks cold," the woman said.

My mother took that as her sign and saw her duty ahead of her. She made the sign of the cross, kissed the old woman's wrinkled cheek, and went outside into the sunshine. She gave my father her address in Trzebinia and walked him to the train station.

On the windowsill here in my father's room, there are three things. A get-well card onto which my mother has glued a picture of the Virgin Mary; a small basket containing a thriving pothos—its big, shiny, green leaves stretching toward the window and sun; and a small, unframed, black-and-white picture of my father—a copy of the photo from his first American passport, the one he had used to go to Poland to find a wife. I have always hated this picture of him. A slight smirk on the lips, something fierce about his eyes. He looks volatile, unpredictable, as if he's about to bark at the photographer.

In the next two months, Dad came to see Mom in Trzebinia four times. Once he came with his brother (for approval), and once he took her to a restaurant where he snapped his fingers and called out to get the waiter's attention. Mom was embarrassed—civilized people didn't do that. On one visit, he asked her if she had a copy of her birth certificate, and she said no, she'd have to go back to her township, and he said, "Maybe the lady should do that soon." He wouldn't tell her why, but that was when she got a feeling. He'd told her up front and early on that he was only there for six months, that he wanted to marry before he returned to America.

On his final visit to her, he asked her for her birth certificate, studied it momentarily, leaning forward with his elbows on his knees. Then he said, "Want to see America?" and she said yes. They were married two days later. They had known each other a grand total of six weeks, had been on five dates, including the night they met, in Kudowa. My father proposed, if you can call that a proposal, on the fifth date.

"Why do you think I tell you this now?" my mother asks me.

"So I never make any major life decisions within six months of severe head trauma?"

She shakes her head, her rough-cut bangs falling behind the smudged lenses of her glasses. She cuts her hair herself and sends the money she'd spend at Supercuts to starving African children. She slides her bangs out with one finger.

"No," she says firmly, lightly slapping her palms against her thighs. "I am serious. I tell you because I know. I know what it's like to have a child too late. By time I had you, I was too old to be mother. You could have had problems." She shakes her head. "I prayed every day I carried you." She reaches for a tissue from the top of the TV and dabs at her eyes.

"Hey," I say, leaning forward and smiling. "Hey, I turned out okay." I wiggle my ten fingers at her. "Mostly, anyway." I hesitate, then add quietly, "And it's not like you had a choice."

"I know," she says, blowing her nose. "But I was still scared. Have babies now, while you are young, strong."

"Things are different now, Mom. They have genetic tests. They can tell if the baby has problems, and then they can—you know...." But I don't say more because abortion is something we don't talk about. If I had one, I wouldn't tell her. And if I did, she'd spend the rest of her life praying for my soul.

"I've got a lot to accomplish before I have kids. I'm still practically a kid myself."

"Not anymore, Magda. Twenty-seven is not 'kid.'"

I don't tell her that I've found a nest of gray hairs near the back of my neck, at the nape. I discovered it blow-drying my roots—the force of the air plastered the outer layers of my hair up against the scalp and there was that little spot in the mirror, shimmering like Christmas tinsel. For a minute, I thought it was just the sunlight—sometimes it makes individual strands of my hair look blonde. But when I turned my head, expecting the sun's reflection to move too, the shimmering remained. And those hairs looked more unruly, more wiry. I made Sam yank them out one by one. "I'm sorry, I'm sorry," he said with each yank. "Tell me when you want me to stop." In the mirror, I saw his thick, straight brows draw together beneath the upper edge of his glasses, the tender, contrite expression of a mother ripping a Band-Aid off a child's knee.

"Get them all," I said. "Don't stop until they're all gone."

My mother got married at the courthouse in a dove gray skirt and jacket. Her brother was there because he lived an hour away in Katowice but it happened too fast for her parents or sisters to come. Afterwards, she served coffee and tea and pastries in her apartment and Dad gave her a silver dollar as a wedding present and two days later he left for America. The next time she heard from him was a year later, when he sent her a ticket and told her to come. English wasn't taught in Polish schools yet, and private tutors were expensive and rare. The only words she could say were "airport," "please," and "bathroom."

She had a layover in London and arrived in San Francisco the next day in her gray wedding suit and stockings and high heels, carrying one brown suitcase. It was two in the afternoon on a Saturday. My father picked her up in the rattling old Buick with no back window and no back seat—just bare, rusted steel where the seat should have been. Without the window, the freeway's roar in the car was so loud that he didn't hear her when she tried to ask him questions about the house he was taking her to, the buildings they zoomed past, and the tall, branchless trees growing here and there along the freeway. Tall like poles with an explosion of fronds on top. She'd never seen anything like them before.

He parked in front of a two-story brown and white house with a carport, a carriage drive, and a huge live oak in the front yard. The house was as big as she'd imagined, and she was breathless. What would her girlfriends say? Her girlfriends who stood in long, wearying lines for bread and rough, brown toilet paper. She would write them letters, try to keep the tone humble, but she'd slip it in somehow, tell them how hard it was to find good furniture to fill such a big house, even here, even in the land of plenty.

"How many bedrooms, Witek?" she asked. He had already gotten out of the car and was marching up the driveway to the front door. He was jangling his keys. The bunch was huge, like a jailer's. She struggled to yank her suitcase out of the backseat, steadying herself in her high heels.

That afternoon, her new husband would tell her to change out of her wedding suit and heels into an old pair of his work pants, cinched around her waist with rope, and one of his V-neck undershirts, yellow sweat stains under the arms. She'd tie a kerchief around her head and she would clean all four of the boarder's rooms upstairs, scrubbing their bathrooms on her hands and knees, soaking her seamstress hands in ammonia and bleach.

She would vacuum and dust and change the sheets, and then she would do the same thing downstairs, just as she would for the next twenty-five years, in her own home and in neighborhood homes, earning the money she placed in her husband's outstretched hand when she came home. The next day, Sunday, he would give her a pair of tall rubber boots and a spade and would wave his hand at the long stretch of dirt in the backyard.

"What about church?" she would ask. And he'd say, "If you want to go, find it yourself." She would spend the afternoon overturning the weed-sprung soil of the backyard, reciting Mass to herself under her breath while he rested on a chair in the winter sunshine. He wanted a vegetable garden.

Lafu, the Tongan nursing assistant, comes in to my father's room, her long dark braid swinging down her back. When she crouches beside Dad's urine pouch, the tip of her braid grazes the carpet. She uncaps the valve and empties Dad's urine into a plastic jug. She holds it up to eye level, squints at the notches in the plastic, and says, "500 milliliters." She wears my mother's handiwork around her neck, a deep eggplant.

My mother reaches for the notepad on which she tracks all of Dad's bodily functions and medication doses. It is her sixth notebook. She's been doing this every day for one year and three months.

Lafu comes out of the bathroom, carrying the now-empty jug, rinsed clean, water droplets clinging to its sides. "Your mother," she says to me, "so devoted. Like saint."

"Yes," I say. "I know." I force myself to smile and then part the curtains, look out at the two redwood trees growing near the corner of the block. They make me think of giant chess pieces, tall and conical.

Mom smiles. "I just pray he gets better. That is all that matters."

"You have to take care of yourself too," Lafu says, and looks at me as if it is my responsibility to make her. I nod. I want to pull on the ends of the scarf that my mother spent two days knitting for her, yank them until they are tight around her throat and she gasps for air.

"If he is okay, then I am okay," Mom says, patting Dad's arm. Lafu closes the door behind her as she leaves. Outside, two brown-winged, orange-bellied birds dive and plummet around each other in the grass between the L-shaped building and the sidewalk. I wonder if they are fighting or courting.

I drop the curtain and say, a little sharply, "You never leave this room. How can I ever get married if my own mother won't come to the wedding?"

She ignores me, smiles patiently, pats Dad's arm. Glances at his chest. It hasn't risen or fallen in almost half a minute. She tugs up on one half of his body, jump-starting him out of his apnea. He doesn't wake but makes a loud, ratchety snort.

"I've got so much more living to do, Mom."

"Sam isn't like *Tata*."

"What? I know that. I'm talking about responsibility, being tied down." Did she think I was waiting for Sam to hand me a pair of his old pants and a spade and motion with one arm to the little plot of a backyard behind his townhouse and then go inside and crack a beer and watch a soccer game on TV?

I have found myself the nicest possible man. The kind of man who lets me be mean to him, who just blinks a little owlishly behind his glasses and smiles patiently when I snap, "When did elbow patches hit the runways again?" after he shows me a new sport coat I didn't help pick out.

"Time is one thing you do not have," my mother says, and I look up at her. But she isn't looking at me. She's looking at my father. He's still asleep. And I'm still glad.

Then she turns to me, reaches over, and rubs the blue scarf between her thick, arthritis-bent fingers. "The blue goes with your eyes," she says, "but the maroon—with your skin." Her eyes roam over my face, looking at all the individual parts of it, my nose, my cheekbones, my lips. She used to do that when I was little. I would squirm out of her grasp, suddenly shy.

I stand up from the pink vinyl chair and look in the mirror again. "I don't know. I can't decide."

"Take both," she says.

"I can't take both. They're for homeless people."

"Give one to Sam."

"I told you, Mom. He doesn't wear scarves."

"Then keep both. Maybe you meet someone who does."

I look at her sharply. But she's picked up her knitting needles again.

When she went to pick up the birth certificate at the Bureau of Records in Rzeszów, the young man who worked behind the counter didn't want to give it to her. He wouldn't say why, but he looked in her eyes with an intense, sudden stare and said, "Really, miss? Are you sure?"

He had the most beautiful eyes she'd ever seen on a man. Deep and green and transparent all at once. To this day, she's never seen such eyes, she says.

This she has never told me before, and I know she only tells me now because my father is asleep, because I am wearing two scarves around my neck and I can't decide which one I want, because she is my mother and she wants me to be happy.

"I thought marrying Dad was your homework assignment from God," I say.

She shrugs, a move so flippant for her I hardly recognize it. "Everyone doubts." She reaches up to her neck, to the little gold cross on a chain, and fingers it.

I leave with both scarves in my handbag.

"Give to Sam," my mother urges.

"Mom, how many times do I have to tell you? He doesn't wear scarves. I'll keep it for myself. I'll need both to keep me warm when I'm old and lonely." I ruffle her hair and kiss her cheek.

"Okay, okay," she says. "Keep for yourself. I knit different one for Sam. Brown. He has brown eyes, no?"

In the elevator, I tell myself that even if I do give it to him, it doesn't mean anything. I don't even have to give it to him. He'll never know. Neither will Mom. I can hear her already, "Sam, how you like your scarf? Keep you warm?"

Last Christmas Eve, I took Sam to visit my parents at the nursing home. I brought my mother a Christmas gift since she wouldn't be with the rest of us to open presents. I gave her a set of four coffee mugs painted with roosters.

She opened them and laughed. "I will be rich!" she said. "Maybe I will win lottery." Then she immediately took two out of the box and handed one to Sam, one to me. "Keep."

"Mom, no." I held the mug back out to her, eyeing Sam to do the same. "These are for you. They're a gift." She gave everything away.

Sam looked to me, unsure of what to do. I smiled, thinking, don't take it, please don't take it.

"Take," my mother urged. "Take, Sam, take. I do not need four. I save one for me, one for *Tata*." Sam thanked her and turned the mug over and over in his hands.

I dangled my cup by its handle. I didn't mean to drop it, but

I did; it slipped out of my hands, thunked on the carpeted floor, and rolled slightly.

"Oh, *Jezu!*" my mother said. She was too kind to scold me for carelessness. She bent and reached for it. After she handed it to me, my mother pressed her hand against the small of her back. She winced, then ignored the pain. With a bright voice, she said, "See? You lucky already."

Witness

I look around the dining room: Dad, Mr. Williams, the bird lady, and a little old man I've never seen before. Roberta, one of the nurses' aides, sweeps plastic trays off the tables, dumps the little plastic dishes and wrappers into a big, blue garbage can in the center of the room. Sometimes she clears the patients' trays before they're done eating. I try to smile at her when she leans over me to take Dad's tray. I wouldn't want to work here either.

Dad was sleeping in his chair, clutching a food-encrusted plastic fork and spoon when I walked in, but I've woken him up. I want him to know I came. He gives me the tiniest, fleeting smile. Each day when I arrive, he looks at me hopefully, expectantly, as if today's the day I'm telling him it's time to go home. But when all I say is, "I like that shirt they put on you today. That's a pretty plaid," he looks away, stares at the flecked wallpaper.

When he first came here, a couple of months ago, I tried to lighten his long hours of boredom by reading to him. For the past few years he had been nagging me to read more Polish, so I brought *Pan Tadeusz*. But when I read the first paragraph, his eyes teared up, and he twisted his lips and tapped his index finger to his temple, the way he used to do to Mom when he was convinced she'd thrown a bill out with the trash. I looked from the Polish text to the English translation on the left side. *My country, thou art like good health. I never knew till now, how precious till I lost thee.*

Now I come earlier, around dinner, so at least I can comment on the food. Those peaches look good, don't they? You always liked canned peaches. And I can make sure Roberta doesn't take his tray before he's done.

Cars pass on University Avenue below. I touch the flowers in a tiny white ceramic vase on the table. Small orange-and-pink-tinged stargazers, purplish carnations. Mr. Williams is parked by the window, punching his arms straight up into the air over his head and then punching straight out in front of him, like a boxer warming up in the corner of the ring. He wears the same gray sweatpants and sweatshirt I see him in every day. He mutters to himself or maybe to me. Last week he tried to grab my ass by the elevator.

After Roberta takes the tray, I say a little to Dad in Polish. "How are you feeling? You look good. Nice haircut." My mother cuts Dad's hair now. She brings a special electric haircutting razor to the nursing home once a month. When I was a kid, Dad used to cut my mother's and my hair in the kitchen every couple of months on Friday nights. He'd gone to barber school when he first came to America—something to fall back on if he couldn't find a machinist's job. He told us the whole story each time, joking, jovial, as we dragged the special swivel chair from the basement. But if something had put Dad in a bad mood that day—the deaf German he worked with at the machine shop or Mom's slightly pigeon-toed walk across the kitchen floor—then we clenched the sides of the chair, our backs rigid, as Dad laid the cold metal shears flat against our necks, our foreheads, snip-snipped our wet hair into identical bowl cuts.

I bring Dad a little paper cup of orange juice from the nurse's cart and place it in his hand. He looks at it, sets it away from him. Returns his gaze to the wallpaper. Then at the next table, a voice—"Miss!" I turn around.

"Yes?"

I stand up, go closer to the little man I've never seen before.

"Sit down." He has an accent and I can't tell from where. I laugh, the way I do to fill awkward silences. Usually, it's the Alzheimer's people who call me over to ask questions. Barbara asks me every time I step out of the elevator if I've got fifty cents for the bus, when is the bus coming, I've got the get to the bus, got to get out of here. Then she screams, "Aaaa-dam, Aaaa-dam, come get me. I don't wanna die."

This man has clear plastic tubes stretching from a metal tank by his chair up to his nose. On the outside of the tank is a plastic pouch full of liquid. I can't tell what it is. He leans across the table towards me, says, "This is your grandfather?"

"No, my father."

"Where is he from?"

"Poland."

I glance at Dad. He's watching us now.

The old man nods his head. He has blue-silver eyes, round and pale and watery. His skin is soft and pink, deeply wrinkled. A smooth, bald head ringed in white fuzz. A red-and-white-striped shirt and maroon bathrobe. A tiny, skinny wisp of a man. Brown leather slippers, bare ankles. His eyelashes are white and he has a curved beak of a nose.

"Where are you from?" I ask, though I already know.

"Poland," he says.

"What's your name?"

"Sal Silverstein." He looks me straight in the eye. "I was in Auschwitz." He holds up his arm and pulls up the jacket sleeve. His number is a little blurry around the edges, but the ink is still dark.

"They killed my parents...everyone."

I glance at Dad. He heard. He has paused in his inching struggle to come over. Then he resumes, more jerkily, more intently. I stand up and pull the brake levers on his chair. He hasn't learned how to propel himself properly; maybe he thinks that if he learns how to use the chair, he won't also learn to walk again.

I sit down again beside Sal Silverstein and say quietly, "My Dad was in Auschwitz too."

"He was? Does he have number?" His eyes are questioning, his face scrunched and intent.

"No," I say, "no, he was in the labor camp. He isn't Jewish."

He leans back, nodding, weighing this information, looking at Dad, appraising him. Dad is now halfway over to us. I get up and wheel him over. The nurses say to let him try to do things on his own, but sometimes I can't watch that painfully slow shuffle, pulling himself forward just by inching his feet along, the chair dragging beneath him. Dad has never met another camp survivor in America. I think there are only two left that he remembers from his barracks—

42

they are old and live in Warsaw. They wrote letters until Dad's stroke, and my mother has written to them now, letting them know that Dad can't read or write or speak.

Sal Silverstein holds out his hand to shake, and Dad grips it so tightly that Sal winces.

And then my father starts to cry. Like a little boy. His face all balled up and tears pouring out, his lips curled up high over his gold incisor. I look around for the nurse's aides. I don't want them to think that I've made him cry.

"Don't cry, don't cry," Sal Silverstein says, prying his hand out of Dad's grip. He rubs Dad's arm. The spot, I notice, where if Dad had had a number, it would have been tattooed.

"It is over now. You survived," Sal says. Still Dad cries.

"It does no good to cry. There is always hope." Still, Dad cries.

Finally, Sal leans back in his chair, points with one hand to the number on his arm and says to my father, "I had it worse than you."

The sobbing relents a little. I look down at the floor and smile. That's what Dad used to say to us, to everyone. If he heard us complaining about something, he'd start retelling his escape story, then he'd look confused for a moment. He would run his hand through his dark hair. Even the night before his stroke—by the back door, on my way out of my parents' house—Dad told me, retold me, the story of his dog, the one they had shot in the barnyard. Told it to me even as I backed away from him. His eyebrows were pulled together, his forehead furrowed, trying to figure out why he had to keep taking little steps. Wondering why he found himself in the driveway all of a sudden, next to my car.

Dad wheels himself up to Sal, who fiddles with his hearing aid. While he talks, he taps on it intermittently, tugs on the wire that snakes down to the little box in his robe pocket. Their knees are practically touching. Dad can't get close enough to him. Dad once told me that when he was a boy, there weren't enough beds in his house. He slept in the same bed as his older brother, Tomek, their feet touching for warmth.

Sal says he's been here for three days. Only yesterday did he feel strong enough to leave his room. He talks to me, but occasionally looks over at Dad. Smiles a little. It's hard for him, too, talking to someone who can't talk back.

Dad looks at me intently while Sal and I talk. I avoid his eyes and look at Sal instead.

Sal says his wife has Alzheimer's. Is she here at the nursing home, I ask? No, she is at a different home. They didn't have room for her here. In Poland, she wanted to be a doctor, but then there was the war. A son, Allen, a lawyer in Palo Alto. A daughter, Sarah, a kindergarten teacher in Chicago.

Sal says he has no appetite. My wife—I miss her, he says. Mom has been telling me about the little Russian man on this floor, Misha, the one who won't eat, the one whose wife comes every day at lunch to cry and plead with him. Eat, eat, she begs. She brings him special dishes she'd cooked that morning. He died yesterday.

I tell Sal about the biotech company I work for, the catalog entries I write in my cubicle all day.

Dad looks from me to Sal as I talk. He presses his lips together, frowns. He tugs at his lap belt as if he wants to try to stand up. He can't stand up without me. I ignore him.

Roberta comes to wheel away the bird lady, who is curled up in fetal position in her chair-bed. Her bony knees and shins poke out from under the white sheets. Her small head lolls to one side; she can't keep it up straight. Her eyes are almost always closed, even when her daughter comes to feed her—small spoonfuls of pudding, applesauce, mashed strawberries.

Sal breaks off his sentence to me and barks, "Miss!" at Roberta. I look over. Sal says nothing, but I see that he is looking at the little brown fuzzy sock crumpled on the floor of the dining room where the bird lady's chair-bed has been parked. One of her gnarled white feet pokes out from beneath the sheet. Roberta pauses, gives him a sullen look, then stoops to pick up the sock.

That's when Dad starts whacking me with his good arm. Rapid solid clap-claps against the right side of my body, closest to him. My upper arm, my forearm, my chest. I scoot my chair back, out of reach, as the speech therapist does when Dad starts hitting her.

"What's wrong?" Sal asks me. "What does he want?"

"I don't know," I say. "I think he just needs to go to sleep. Good night, Mr. Silverstein."

Dad's still flailing with his good arm as I push his chair out of the room and down the hall.

***

I arrive at the nursing home later than usual the next night. I've been behind on the catalog deadline and I had to catch up on all the cloning kit entries. I wonder if Dad got enough to eat. I buy a 7up—his favorite—at the vending machine in the downstairs lobby, and then I take the elevator to the second floor. I find him in the TV room already, parked perpendicular to the TV. I flip the brake levers on the wheels and swivel him around so that he can actually see the screen. *Hollywood Squares* is on and no one else is in here.

Dad stares at the upper left corner of the wall, where the spider plant hangs from a hook. I see a thread hanging from one of the "leaves."

I say, "Hi, Dad. How are you feeling today?" He does not turn his head. Just stares at the wall, stone-faced. I put the cold can in his good hand. I get a plastic cup from the nurse's cart. When I return, he is rolling the can over and over in his hand.

"That's great exercise for you," I say. I pull one of the vinyl chairs up so I am sitting next to him in front of the TV. If he could use his hands like he used to, he could open the tab himself. I ask him if he wants me to pour the 7up into the cup for him, and he uncurls his palm. The can thumps the blue-gray carpeting, rolls forward, and bumps the lower edge of the wooden TV console.

I flip through the channels, looking for a nature or history program. He always called sitcoms trash. He told us to turn them off, disgusted. Told us to go read Polish. We were forgetting our Polish.

On Sundays, he made me read ten pages of *Polska Historia* aloud to him. He interrupted when I mispronounced a word. "Do you know what that means?" he'd ask. "Yes," I'd lie. Every time he started to explain what something meant, it invariably led to a story, a story I'd already heard.

When I was in the fifth grade, one of my homework assignments was to write a story. Mine was about a family of pumpkins living in a patch. On Halloween, one of the baby pumpkins is torn away, carved, sent to pumpkin heaven, gets reincarnated as pie. I got an E—*Excellent*. I showed it to Dad. He laughed, shook his head, said, "If you want to write stories, write my story. Someday you tell it to everyone, so they know what I survived."

Now he wants what I won't give him. I look out the window, at the cars passing in the street below. Some of the cars' headlights blink on as they approach the building. It is that time of day—when you must decide if it's gotten dark enough to turn your headlights on.

Sal Silverstein shuffles past the TV room, pulling his green metal tank behind him on a little dolly. Dad jerks and inches toward the door. I wish I'd remembered to put the brakes on. I follow him.

At the doorway, he looks down the hall at Sal's back, at the long, maroon bathrobe.

Dad makes those guttural grunts and murmurs—what he has for language now.

I put my hand on Dad's shoulder. "Dad," I say. "Mr. Silverstein can't hear very well. He won't hear you."

Dad jerks from beneath my hand and continues inching up the hall. The garbled, throaty noises continue.

Sal has stopped, leaned down to adjust one of the dials on his tank, and now Dad inches faster and faster, his whole torso leaning into the momentum of it. I should push him, I should get him there faster. I should call out to Mr. Silverstein.

But it is Mr. Silverstein who calls out to Dad.

"Eh," he says. "You move very fast." He straightens from turning the dial, presses one hand to his back. Holds his other hand out to Dad. Dad takes it and won't let go.

I am hoping that Dad will be content with just holding his hand and staring—he's already begun to cry. But no. He tries to speak. Shakes his head. Starts again. I wonder if it sounds the same to him as it does to us. Or if he sees his meaning in his head, doesn't hear the sound.

I close my eyes and wrap my arms around my chest. But Sal is asking me something.

"What is he saying? What does he want?"

"Dad," I say. "Let Mr. Silverstein go to his room. Maybe he's tired." I lean over Dad's chair and bend down to look him in the eye. He bats at me with his free hand. It is the weaker one, though, and it only brushes my chin. I back up anyway.

"What? What is it?" Sal asks.

I want to run up the hall, get in the elevator, climb into my car, turn the music up loud, sing along. Everyone should be able to say what he needs to say. A drink of water, please. Leave my tray. Here's my story.

"Dad wants me to tell you his story, Mr. Silverstein. How he ended up in Auschwitz, how he survived. He thinks you'll understand."

Sal shakes his head, pats Dad's hand with his own wrinkly

one. "Come into my room."

Sal sits on the edge of his bed, the plastic sidebars lowered. I roll Dad's chair up so that he faces Sal, and I drag a chair up beside him. Silvery get-well balloons bump the ceiling tiles. A bouquet of daisies stands on the night table. Another bouquet—pink carnations and baby's breath—stands on top of the TV.

Sal takes Dad's hand in both of his. "So you want me to know your story. I know without you telling me. It is a story of pain, like mine. It is enough to have lived it once. I do not like to talk about past too much, to hear about it too much. Especially our past. Better to forget. Try to forget." He pushes up his sleeve, holds his arm out. "I can't forget, but you can. Time does everything. Be patient." He pats Dad's hand again, and now Dad just stares at him.

"When I remember, I can't sleep," Sal says. "I have nightmares. Maybe you tell me someday. But not tonight."

I expect Dad to try again, that gurgling, those words like vague dark shapes in the night. You can almost see them, almost make them out, but not quite.

Dad stares. He doesn't even cry.

I pull his chair out of the room. He drags his feet.

"Sorry to have bothered you. Mr. Silverstein," I call as we back through the doorway. "I hope you sleep well. Good night."

When I was in the eighth grade, a Polish physics professor stayed at our house for a week. He was from the Jagiellonian University in Kraków, and he was attending a conference on superconductors at Stanford. He was a friend of some uncle in Poland. On his first night at our house, Dad told him the story, everything, acted it all out in the middle of the kitchen. The yanking from the bed, the marching, the beatings, the escape. The long night in the forest, under the boughs of the fir tree, the long bicycle ride back to his mother's farm. Dad kept the professor up past midnight. The professor yawned, stretched, said what a long day he'd had, but Dad kept going. This story and then this one and the next one.

At the breakfast table, after Dad had already left for work, the physics professor looked into his coffee cup and then at my mother.

"My wife's father was in Auschwitz, too. But he's never mentioned it once. Not to anyone. He came back and never said a word. He won't tell you if you ask."

"Everyone is different," Mom said.

"Yes," the physics professor said. "Everybody is."

The next day, when I arrive at the home after work, the elevator is broken and I have to take the stairs. They are at the side of the building, and when I get up to the second floor, I must pass Sal's room to reach the TV room and the dining room. Sal's name is no longer in the little plastic pouch on the door, and I stop. I knock. No answer. I push open the door. The bed has been stripped. The flowers and balloons are gone. I walk to the nurse's station.

"Carla, what room did Mr. Silverstein move to?"

"He's gone," she says. Gone can mean a lot of things in this place. Mr. Carver, in the room next door to Dad's, died last week. Mom, who sits with Dad until dinnertime, said she heard Mr. Carver coughing for a half hour, calling, "Carla, Carla." Finally, Mom went to go find Carla and bring her back. But the coughing had stopped by the time they returned.

"Gone where?" I ask.

"I don't know," she says. "I came on at noon and his room was already empty." I can ask her to check the books, but I don't. Maybe his wife's place found a room for him.

Dad's in the TV room again.

"Let's see what's going on in the world today, Dad." I turn on CNN. He used to watch the news and read the paper every night at home.

But he won't look at the TV screen. He looks at the wall. Only his face isn't stony today, and when I take his hand, he holds it tightly. I close my eyes.

Then I smell something.

"Dad, I'm going to get Roberta." He doesn't want to let go of my hand but I pry it out anyway.

They'd been digging ditches somewhere, and on the long march back to the barracks, they walked two-by-two. They hadn't eaten in days. Most of them were barefoot. It was November. One of the men saw a dry stump of a cabbage, probably frozen through, in the stubble of a field they passed. He dove for it. Was gunned down before his hands even touched it. His body crumpled, a heap of filthy, striped fabric. The SS-men stopped the march. Lined the twenty-some men up in two rows, the tall ones behind, the shorter ones in front, as if arranging them for a photograph.

Who else wants to die today?

Nobody spoke. My father, sixteen, tried to sniff back the mucus running from his nose.

The SS-man heard him. You? You? He pointed the gun in his face, inches away from my father's nose.

My father shook his head. His life depended on not making a sound, on not crying. There was an unmistakable odor, a wet stain spreading down the front of his pants.

Roberta wheels Dad to his room to change the diaper and then wheels him back. I watch CNN until he reappears in the doorway.

"Thanks, Roberta." She nods, and I pull his chair the rest of the way into the room.

"Dad," I say, "Do you want me to ask Mr. Silverstein if maybe he'd like to listen today? He was tired yesterday. We could ask him again."

Dad nods.

"You wait here. I'll go ask."

I walk up the hall and into Mr. Silverstein's room. I sit on the stripped bed. Count the second hand on my watch. Sixty ticks. I walk back out, down the hall, past the cheap, plastic-framed prints of beach scenes—sunsets or sunrises, up to you.

"Dad, I think Mr. Silverstein was transferred to his wife's nursing home today. Carla said it happened so fast, he didn't have time to say goodbye to you, but he told her to tell you he'd like to hear the story some day. He was sorry yesterday was a bad night for him."

Now he cries, the way he did that first time he saw Mr. Silverstein, in the dining room, two nights ago. I rub his hand. I rub his shoulders. I bring him a cup of orange juice. I bring him a cup of water. I flip the channels of the TV until I find a documentary about

Jacques Cousteau, something about the mysteries of the deep.

Mr. Williams rolls by in the lobby, peers in through the window. Backs up and pokes his head in.

"He okay?"

"Yes, he will be."

I hear Barbara cry out in the hallway. "Aaaa-dam, Aaaa-dam. When are you coming for me?"

I shut the door that separates the TV room from the rest of the floor. Roberta passes the windows, pushing the laundry bin. She looks in. I smile.

I look out the window on the other side. It is already dark, and all the cars have their headlights on. When the light turns green at the intersection, the cars flow past. I turn off the TV.

I reach into my purse, pull out *Pan Tadeusz*. I turn to page two, move my finger down the page, past *how precious till I lost thee*. I let the tip of my finger rest beneath the next sentence. I look up.

This isn't what he wants to hear. But I must say something. I can't just watch this old man stare out the darkened window of a nursing home—a window that no longer shows the world he can't go out into, but only his own body in the wheelchair, his own silent face, his close-cropped hair.

Finally, I fold the corner of the page and reach over to run my fingertips through his hair. He used to tell me how in barber school, he learned how to shave a man, give a head massage, dip combs and shears in jars of antiseptic.

There is the tiniest twist to his mouth. I can't tell if it's a smile.

I remember sitting in the pink-and-orange-flowered swivel chair in the middle of the kitchen, wearing the pinstriped barber's smock, toilet paper wound tight around my neck so the clippings wouldn't slip down my shirt. Squinting, clenching the arms of the chair, holding my breath as Dad snips my bangs and tells my mother to walk like a normal person, feet straight, not like some cripple from the countryside, even though he knew that's all she was anyway.

I tuck *Pan Tadeusz* back in the purse at my feet. "Dad," I say, straightening up in my chair. "Dad, remember those haircuts you used to give us? I remember them. I remember everything."

Survivors

When I was two years old, my father went fishing on the Tracy River with his Ukrainian friend. A dead cat lay in the middle of the levee road. She had been hit by a car, and her kittens swarmed her body—some still sucking her teats, some circling, meowing. When my father tried to catch them, most of them scattered. He scooped up two—one black and one orange. He brought them home, and I remember the excitement: dusk and kittens on our back porch steps. The black one he gave to the friend. The orange one he kept for us and named Rusty.

My mother and father grew up on farms in Poland, where animals were not pets. Dogs came closest: there was a dog on my father's farm—a smart dog, he said. Only once did Kukusz bark when he shouldn't have: when the SS-men's truck rumbled into through my grandmother's barnyard. Kukusz barked and barked, straining and leaping at the end of his chain. One of the SS-men shot him dead. Then they led my father, at gunpoint, past Kukusz's body and loaded him onto a truck.

On my father's farm, cats were exclusively for catching mice; they were neither fed nor allowed in the house. They were considered in cahoots with the devil because they wouldn't shy away from a dead body the way a dog would. A cat would sniff it and paw at it and God knows what else. I do not know if this is true. I know that my father was taught to believe that redheaded children were kin of the devil, as were left-handed children. In elementary school, my father was trained to write with his right hand, though for everything else, he was left-handed. Until he had a stroke in his seventies and could no longer write, he had lovely penmanship. His letters were well crafted, artful: all straight lines and corners and angles. He wrote slowly, deliberately, with a kind of calligraphic concentration.

Rusty was not allowed in the house. I was told to wash my hands every time I touched him and to shoo him away from the back door, which he scratched up significantly. Far too late in the game, my father affixed a long strip of plexiglass to the back door so Rusty would simply slide down, meowing and pawing.

I don't remember my father ever petting Rusty. He did occasionally stick out his work boot or—if it was a Sunday—his wingtip for Rusty to nuzzle. This was rare. Usually, when he passed Rusty in the driveway, he whipped out his arm and lunged to startle him, and made a sound like kccccccchhhhh. Rusty always fled.

I was not very kind to Rusty in his sleep either, but for different reasons. Rusty was growing old as I was growing up. By the time I turned sixteen, Rusty was stiff and arthritic and grouchy. I was scared he would die in his sleep. So when I saw him lying motionless on the patio flagstones, I tiptoed toward him and clapped my hands loudly above his head. He was never dead.

Once, my parents discovered a family of mice that had carved out a nest in the back of the old radio my father had brought with him from Europe, but by the time my mother went to get the cat, the mice had scattered throughout the house. We did have rats in the garage—big, squirrel-sized ones—but Rusty had seemed to work out an arrangement with them. He refrained from killing them, and they showed themselves infrequently.

I know it was hard for my father to see my mother put sacks of cat food in the shopping cart, but he did not stop her. And Rusty did get one visit to the vet—for neutering—when my father first brought him home. But no matter how much Rusty bled or how badly he limped from fights with the neighborhood cats, he did not go to the vet again. Doctors were for people, not animals, my father said, and there was nothing we could do about it.

The most famous incident of my father and the cat is

this: one late evening, my father sat on the toilet in the downstairs bathroom, a few feet away from the back door. It was a cold night; Rusty scratched, my father yelled. My father stumbled into the laundry room with his pants around his ankles, newspaper rolled up in hand. He opened the back door and lunged out onto the back porch, swearing. He thwacked Rusty's haunch once and chased him all the way out to the end of the driveway, where my father tripped and hit his head on the pavement. His pants were still around his ankles. My mother dabbed iodine onto the wound on my father's forehead with an appropriate expression of concern, but when she turned away from him to put the bottle back on the top shelf of the medicine cabinet, I saw her smiling.

Immediately following the newspaper incident, Rusty dove under the woodpile, which was elevated by cinderblocks so the wood wouldn't rot on the soil. Every day after school, I knelt in the dirt in front of the woodpile and peered beneath the wood. I saw his eyes glint, gold-green, and I knew he had not run away, at least. Nothing would lure him out, not even leftover trout or chicken slathered in raw egg.

"I hate Dad," I said to my mother.

"You think you do," she said, "but he's your father, and you love him even if you think you don't." I found this infuriating. Surely, the decision to give and receive love was mine to make. Also, I didn't believe her. She had seemed to make some kind of a pact with God. When my father did something I knew in my bones was wrong— hitting the cat, calling my mother a cripple for her pigeon-toed gait—I fumed and scribbled in my journal. But my mother didn't even seem ruffled. Instead, she smiled. Many years later, I asked her how she managed to be so patient. She said she recited Hail Marys until she could see the vision that usually came to her: the Blessed Mother in green rubber garden boots stepping high over a pile of shit.

After the newspaper debacle, my mother began letting Rusty into the house in the mornings, while my father was at work, and I shooed him out before four, when my father came home. If my father's truck rolled up the driveway and the cat was still inside, both of us made a mad dash for the closest exit. Rusty went through windows, side doors, back doors—once even through an upstairs window onto the porch roof and down the trunk of the almond tree.

As Rusty got even older, my mother could see that his joints had become stiff, that he had arthritis just as she did, and that the cold winter nights aggravated it. She lined a cardboard box with thick yellow foam, old blankets, and tattered pillows, and placed it in a corner of the garage. She trained him to sleep in it by scattering chunks of chicken meat slipped from her own plate for a few days. And then, a few months after that, my mother began making him a hot water bottle and carrying it out to him at night.

The first time she prepared the hot water bottle, my father said, "What a waste of water. He's got a fur coat. You baby him, like those American women and their little dogs." So the next night, my mother heated the water in the kettle after my father had gone to bed. She filled the hot water bottle and put it at the foot of her own twin bed, across the room. "*Ja*," my father said. "That's right. Make me one, too." She said the other hot water bottle had sprung a leak some time ago; they'd have to buy another. Then she said she'd better check the back door lock one more time, and quickly, she snuck the second hot water bottle out to the garage, where she tucked it into Rusty's bed. She did this every night for the remaining years of Rusty's life—even summer nights, because the air was cool and damp.

Rusty grew stiff and old and awkward, snaggletoothed and nearly blind. He stayed skinny, no matter how many raw eggs my mother cracked for him. He no longer bothered licking his coat until it gleamed. Occasionally, he veered toward a squirrel in the front yard or batted a paw at a moth flitting about his nose—but always halfheartedly, as if some predatory feline instinct continued to motor inside him, but about which he cared little. Still, if my father was watching through the big picture window in the living room when Rusty went through the motions of pouncing on a squirrel, my father seemed impressed. "A survivor," he'd say. "Look at him."

One afternoon when I was away at college, Rusty wandered away from home. He had not been eating much lately, even though my mother bought canned food for him on the sly. She opened the can in the garage, transferred half the contents into a bowl for the next day, and immediately tossed the can into the trash container by the garage. Once my father mistook the bowl in the refrigerator for some kind of meat stew and sopped it up cold with a slice of bread. My mother said nothing—just smiled, looked toward the ceiling.

After two weeks, Rusty wandered back, rickety and skeletal, stuck all over with burrs and leaves and dirt. He nuzzled up against my mother's legs as she watered the garden. My mother kneeled on the ground and gently tugged each and every burr from his coat. She cracked raw eggs for him, opened a can of salmon. My mother held the food dish close to his nose in case he could neither see nor smell. He sniffed but would not eat. He curled up in a corner of the backyard, near the bamboo-infested chicken coop that had once been ringed with chicken wire for the very purpose of keeping him out. He meowed feebly once or twice and did not get up again until my mother picked him up and took him inside. She called a neighbor to drive her to the vet for Rusty's second and last visit, and she cried the whole way there and back and in bed, too, after out of habit she'd taken the hot water bottle to the garage and tucked it into a cardboard bed that would remain forever empty.

While my mother lay in bed, crying silently, she stayed quiet while my father told her again the story of the cat's survival and the part he'd played in it. "Oh, shut up, shut up tonight," she said.

My father, who had long ago figured out the other bottle went to the cat but had said nothing all those years, waited a moment before saying, "Eh, mother, my feet are cold, you make me a bottle tonight." My mother did not reply. "Did you hear me?" he said.

"Get it yourself," she said very quietly. Her heart thumped, but nothing happened. Within a minute that felt like an hour that felt like a year, my father began snoring. My mother, I realize now, pronounced her defiance so quietly that either my father didn't hear her or, suddenly understanding the dangerous unpredictability of the grief-stricken, wisely decided to say nothing at all.

Oysters

The summer before I left for college, Miss Pierce began pulling weeds topless. On warm days, she stood in her front yard in a bra and polyester slacks, gray hair always in curlers, hands on hips. She surveyed the neighborhood, occasionally bending to yank out a weed, one hand pressed to the small of her back. When I crossed the street to pick up her grocery list on Friday afternoons, she led me into the kitchen and sat across from me, wiping her eyes when her own stories made her cry and tucking the tissues between her bra cups.

Every week she asked when I was leaving and I said September. Already she'd asked me a couple of times if I would come home on weekends. I knew she worried about how she'd get her groceries done, since she didn't have a car. She never asked about my mother because we both knew she couldn't help. Besides, my father didn't even like to see my mother talking to Miss Pierce on the sidewalk. Miss Pierce had been divorced for decades.

In August, college and freedom still seemed a long way off. I started telling my parents I was going to the library to get a head start on calculus, and instead I biked to the restaurant where Clara worked. She stood behind a tiled counter on the patio in front of the restaurant and served wine and oysters to customers waiting for their tables. Each time I visited, she pulled an oyster out of the ice bucket and waved it in front of my face. Shellfish was my least favorite food—a distaste I'd inherited from my mother. Show my mother a package of frozen shrimp in the grocery store and she immediately shuddered, closed her eyes, and pressed her hands to her stomach.

Clara's parents had finally divorced the previous winter, and her mother had begun picking her up from my house with different men in the car. Her hair color seemed to change with the passenger, too. One week, she would be a bronzy redhead; another, a platinum blonde. One Saturday after Clara had gone home, my father called me over to his chair and lectured me on the fall of the American family. By summer, he decided I couldn't be friends with Clara. He never thought to bar me from doing Miss Pierce's grocery shopping. He wouldn't begrudge me the chance to earn some money for college, though Miss Pierce kept me at a steady rate of two dollars a week the entire six years I worked for her.

I could have recited on command the story of Miss Pierce's failed marriage: a friend had seen Miss Pierce's husband leaving another woman's apartment one day at noon. There was no mistaking what that was about. Miss Pierce told other stories, too: the stepfather who beat her older brothers but bought her penny-candies, life as a salesgirl at Bergdorf's in Chicago, the fox-fur coat she'd bought on layaway but couldn't wear after she saw it on a black woman she passed in the street. And her beautiful, jet-haired, green-eyed friend who got syphilis and shot herself in a New York high-rise. When she first told me that story, I was in the seventh grade. I didn't know what syphilis was.

In Miss Pierce's kitchen, I learned to tell time without looking at my watch. I could sense forty-five minutes in the pressure of my thighs on the vinyl seat, in the slant of light coming in through the blinds. I sat on one of the yellow chairs with the cold chrome legs and toed the little black crescents where the chair had scuffed the linoleum. There was no point in looking at her clock—it had stopped long ago.

That last summer Miss Pierce's stories began melding into one another, shape-shifting. Sometimes her green-eyed friend shot herself in a blue-silk negligee in the next-door apartment. Sometimes Miss Pierce bought her fox-fur coat in San Francisco instead of Chicago. Sometimes her husband left her instead of the other way around.

In June, Miss Pierce said, "I might be leaving, too." She reached into her shirt, pulled out the rumpled tissue. "Mavis. You know."

Every couple of months during that time, I had seen a blue Volvo station wagon in Miss Pierce's driveway, and I knew her niece was visiting from Stockton. Mavis was a tiny, trim woman with short gray hair, huge eyeglasses, and a firm handshake. She had two teenage sons and worked full-time at the post office. When I met her, she was making a cheese and mayonnaise sandwich at the kitchen counter. She said hello and disappeared into Miss Pierce's living room.

"I don't want to be nobody's burden," Miss Pierce had told me, loud enough for Mavis to hear. She added, in a whisper, "And I don't want people getting in my business."

For someone who didn't want people getting in her business, Miss Pierce knew a lot about the neighbors. The couple who had just moved into the gray-shingled cottage to her left owned a zippy red convertible and planted a Japanese maple in their backyard. The man raised his voice at night and the woman wore heels so high sometimes she tottered down the sidewalk. The Warners lived to the right: Miss Pierce thought Mrs. Warner was a little nosy and she was sure that Mr. Warner swept the leaf debris from his driveway onto hers early in the morning. I envisioned her spending the day leaning over the kitchen sink and parting the blinds with her bony finger, scanning the street up and down for news.

She knew what went on at our house, too. "I know what kind of a man your father is. He's used to being waited on hand and foot. I can tell he doesn't like me. He knows I wouldn't stand for that."

It was true. When my father banned my mother from speaking to Miss Pierce, he said, "I don't want her putting ideas into your head."

"There's not much you can do with a man like that except divorce him or outlive him," Miss Pierce told me. "And your mother isn't the kind to divorce."

That last Friday in August, I biked slowly up Miss Pierce's driveway, her two grocery bags heavy in the wire baskets over my rear wheel, making my bike lean first this way, then that. It was still warm, the trees thick with leaves. It wouldn't be fall—my favorite season—until Halloween. But I'd be gone when the kids came trick-or-treating through my neighborhood, ringing doorbells the way Clara and I once had. We never rang Miss Pierce's doorbell. No one did. On Halloween, she turned out her lights and went to bed early.

She had left the gate unlocked for me, and I pushed it open with my foot, a bag in each arm. I called out her name and she unbolted the back door and let me in. I usually put the food out on her counter and folded up the bags while she looked over the receipt and counted the change. But that evening, when she shuffled into the back of the house to get my money, the phone rang from somewhere I couldn't see. "Hello, Mavis," I heard her say. I opened the refrigerator to put in the milk.

"I know why you're calling and I haven't changed my mind."

There were a lot of half-gallons of milk in there—six, maybe seven. The expiration dates went all the way back to June. I looked over my shoulder, then pulled out a carton—heavy, nearly full.

I noticed the stack of cheddar cheese packages. Several cartons of eggs. I opened the freezer. Stacks of peas, towers of spaghetti dinners, styrofoam trays of frozen chicken breasts. In the breadbox on the counter, five loaves of sourdough, slices spilling out from some of the opened packages. One package at the back bulged with waves and ridges of mold.

"I told you before. You'll have to come down here and drag my dead body."

In the cupboards above the counter: fourteen cans of peaches, three crumb-coffee rings.

"Mavis, I'm going to go now." I heard the phone bang, and I jumped. I shut the cupboard door and turned around.

"I'm sorry about that," Miss Pierce called. "That woman is always nagging at me." I heard her slippers shush-shushing the floorboards and then she came through the kitchen doorway, holding my money out to me.

"Thank you, honey. See you next week?"

I was never the sort of girl who felt comfortable touching people—Clara and I had never hugged and we'd been best friends since fifth grade—but the way Miss Pierce looked at me told me I had to do something. When I put my arms around her, she stiffened, then softened. "Oh, honey," she said. "You sweet girl." She smelled like baby powder and bad breath, and when I felt her bones tighten around me, I pulled away too quickly.

I passed the knee-high weeds of her yard and looked at the sky. There was a crescent moon and an hour-and-a-half of daylight left. I biked down the darkening streets, my helmet dangling off my handlebars.

The restaurant was busy and the patio was crowded—Clara poured glass after glass of wine. I sat on a stone bench under planters full of geraniums and waited for the crowd to die down. Then Clara slid me an empty 7up can filled with chardonnay. She held out an oyster and I took it, tipped the shell to my lips. I ate oysters and washed each one down with the wine. When the boys hooted from their cars, we rolled our eyes, but when Clara dared me to shout, "Come and get it," I did.

Clara threw a cork at me and I threw it back, and then a pocket of late diners flooded the patio, and I knew I had to go home, knew I had to tell my mother what I'd seen in Miss Pierce's cupboards. I had a queasy feeling in my stomach, and during the whole ride home I wanted to turn around and go back to the patio where people were eating and laughing and having fun. Every time I passed under a streetlight, I made a wish.

American Cousin

While my mother peeled potatoes and drank cup after cup of tea in glass tumblers at my aunt's house all summer, my cousin Ewa and I drank beer at the Arab's bar. It was upstairs, one small smoky room with a pool table and two purple-curtained windows overlooking the train station. There was a narrow, black counter with a low wooden overhang and four barstools. The toilet was behind a black curtain on a rod. The night the Arab told me his wife was coming to meet me, I went behind that curtain and splashed cold water on my face. Ewa and I had been there since two in the afternoon, and we'd long since stopped counting our drinks. When I came out from behind the curtain, the Arab glanced up and tilted the vodka bottle toward my glass. I shook my head and asked for a Pepsi.

Not even Ewa knew the Arab's real name. He wasn't an Arab; he was Polish. But everyone in Ewa's village called him the Arab because of his dark skin and hair. He had a naturally darker complexion than anyone else, even the farmers who worked in the sun all day. "He's almost black," Ewa said to me on one late-night walk home. "Don't you think so?" Ewa had never seen a black person other than on TV. "Bill Cosby?" she said, and pronounced it "Beel." When I told her that black kids from Oakland had been bused to my school in Palo Alto, Ewa's eyes widened. Then she shrugged. "People are people," she said. She scrunched her coppery hair with both hands. Her girlfriends called her "Ruda"—redhead. Everyone had nicknames. Ewa's friend Marcin, who helped out at the Arab's bar, was called Trobek, short for wątroba, or liver, because he drank so much. He must have an extra, the Arab said to me once, and winked.

"*Kuzynko*, your last night." Ewa clinked her tumbler to my Pepsi bottle and looked at me steadily for a moment, then smiled. She narrowed her eyes and glanced around the bar. She was going to be a superb farmer—that careful squint, already practiced at calculating long rows of potato plants, those strong arms, that cowboy swagger that I was sure she learned from John Wayne movies though she claimed she'd never seen one.

"Tonight," Ewa said, nodding her head. "Tonight we find you someone." I was eighteen and had never been kissed. Even after a year of college. "*Jezu*, no time to waste," Ewa had said after I confessed.

Trobek had finished carrying the crates up—vodka, Fanta, Pepsi—and sat down at a table. He was unemployed and lived at home with his parents, like everyone else Ewa's age in that town. Trobek had long, olive lashes, acne-scarred cheeks, and short, brown, buzz-cut hair. He hardly spoke, barely looked me in the eye. But after the Arab poured him a drink, he got lively, teased me about being the Amerikanka.

I wore loose tunics and pants with elastic waistbands that summer—even dug my mother's pants out of her suitcase when all of my own pants were dirty. I had been eating dorm food for a year and now my aunt's home-cured meats and lard-fried potatoes. The only time I felt beautiful was when I danced with the Arab. The first thing he'd said to me when Ewa introduced us was, "*Ale babsko.*" What a broad. It's a compliment, Ewa whispered. Don't worry.

The Arab kept a jar of pickles in the fridge, and every night Trobek ate them while he drank. When the Arab refused to pour him any more drinks, he pulled his flask out of his back pocket, and not long after that the Arab locked the door to the stairway and pulled the curtains, and the four of us danced until we had sweat almost all the vodka out of our pores. Then Ewa grabbed my arm, slapped the Arab's hands off both of us, and said, "It's already two! Your mother!" And laughing, arms linked and tripping over each other, we ran through town and past the tall, concrete *bloki*, past the courthouse and the stone church, past the cemetery where our grandfather was buried, and down the dark lane leading out of town. Dogs yipped and snarled at us from behind fences, and I was sure I'd die by Polish-dog-attack. Sometimes the dogs worked their way through the fences and darted toward us. They were fierce, tightly wound little things that nipped at our ankles. Ewa threw rocks at them. I shrieked and hopped around.

My mother's right calf had been mangled by a dog on that very lane when she was fourteen, walking to church. Ever since then, she'd worn tights and long skirts or pants to hide the shiny, scarred skin. Back home, she'd taught me to cross the street anytime an unaccompanied dog trotted towards us on the sidewalk. I had never had a dog for a pet, though my father had bought one years ago as a subtle message to my mother to get on with what would become my "miracle" birth. It died before I was born.

In the mornings, Ewa and I came to the table with headaches and queasy stomachs. My mother frowned at us, lips pressed thin, while Ewa's mother slid bowls of *barszcz* in front of us with halfhearted reproof on her sister's behalf. Ewa's father, eating "second breakfast" before going back to the fields, smiled, winked, and whispered into my ear, "Were there boys?"

I hadn't been allowed to date in high school, and when I left for college, my father reminded me that school was the most important thing. Boys could come later. My mother didn't say anything, but many times she'd told me the story of her youngest sister, the one who worked as a bakery clerk in Gdańsk because she'd never finished high school: she was expelled in 1967, when she was sixteen. The principal had seen her in a coffeehouse with a boy.

There was a shoebox full of cassettes on top of the Arab's bar, but most of the time he played the one I'd brought with me—a mixtape made by a boy in my AP Biology class our senior year. I knew he had a crush on me; he'd called me the night before Christmas break and asked me to meet him halfway between his house and mine. He knew I wasn't allowed to date—everyone knew—so it saved me the horror of having to explain. After my parents were in bed and asleep, I sprinted two blocks to meet the boy in the cold street; he hugged me so hard, he seemed like a different creature than the shy, quiet, lanky kid who sat at my lab bench. I ran all the way back home, agapanthus leaves slapping my jeans. I could still smell his leather jacket on my arms even when I was back in bed, listening to the tape on my Walkman, the window wide open beside me.

The Arab loved the tape the first time I played it and asked to keep it. It was good: Dire Straits, Peter Gabriel, Tom Petty. The Arab knew enough English to point at me and smile the first time he heard "American Girl." And then he bowed—formally, with a flourish—and asked me to dance.

I taught Ewa and the Arab to dance the way other kids danced at dorm-room parties. Ewa and the Arab called it "dirty dancing." Patrick Swayze was immortal in Poland. So was Mickey Rourke. Ewa owned a pirated copy of *Wild Orchid* and made me watch it with her over and over on the upstairs TV.

The Arab was a good dancer—the best of the four of us. He danced with everyone—Ewa, her friends when they came to the bar, but mostly with me. He was shorter than I was, and stocky. He almost always wore black pants and a light green, short-sleeved, button-down shirt with dark stains under the arms. He smelled like sweat and cigarettes. When he danced with me in the little space between the pool table and the barstools, he got close, his arms around me, his hands at the small of my back, sometimes delving into the waistband of my borrowed pants, or up my shirt. He ripped my bra once. I didn't know until I undressed—as quietly as I could in the wood-paneled room I shared with my mother. By the moonlight coming in over the potato fields, I saw the giant tear in the white lace near the clasp, the underwire needling out from its protective binding. I stuffed the bra deep into my suitcase. The next morning, I showed it to Ewa. She smiled. "Our Casanova," she said.

That last night in the bar, the Arab announced that his wife, Agatka, was coming to meet me before I left for America. She was bringing the baby. Around eight we all heard a high, birdlike call outside the window. "Marek, Marek!"

The Arab put down his drink and came around the side of the counter.

I looked at Ewa. "Marek?"

She shrugged. "Now we know his name, at least."

When he came clunking back up the stairs, he carried a navy blue stroller, a little girl inside it, no older than one, laughing.

His wife was pretty—small, with curly blonde hair, a sharp chin, and a narrow, delicate nose. Her eyes were rimmed in blue eyeliner and thick mascara. She wore a polyester dress that draped over her breasts and middle and thighs in an eye-jarring swirl of lime and kelly green. When I looked away, the pattern remained imprinted in my eyes. It was the sort of dress my mother used to purchase by the armload at the Salvation Army to send to my aunt. I noticed a little bit of fraying at the hem, a long white thread clinging to Agatka's nude nylons. Her legs looked almost brown in them.

She wore high heels and lipstick, and when we shook hands, I noticed her hand was small and soft, but she held tight—so tight it hurt. We kissed cheeks, both sides. I smelled powder and perfume.

"Agatka wanted to meet the Amerikanka," the Arab said. He poured vodka into a tumbler and set it in front of Agatka.

"And she's as pretty as they say." Agatka squeezed my hand once more, hard, then let go. "And why shouldn't she be—she's Polish. Or half-Polish." She reached for her drink.

I responded politely to Agatka's questions: my parents, school, plans for the future. She leaned over the stroller when the baby fussed, but she looked around the bar instead of at the baby. Then she spoke to the Arab. "Busy today?" she asked. "Lots of customers? Or just young ladies?" He didn't answer.

Ewa and Trobek played pool. I wanted to join them but felt stuck at the bar, almost as if I were Agatka's guest, or Agatka mine. I was scared that when the Arab got home at night, beneath his liquor-stench, Agatka smelled my soap or shampoo or sweat. When the Arab refilled Agatka's glass, I pushed mine forward as well.

Agatka lifted her glass. "To your safe travel tomorrow." She drank two to my one, held her glass out to the Arab over and over again, and the Arab refilled it, more reluctantly each time. Eventually, he refused.

"Free drinks for all the girls except your own wife?" She laughed, one harsh sound. She looked at me, and I tried to smile. I held my index finger out to the little girl, and instead of grabbing hold of it, she wailed.

The Arab told Agatka to take the baby home, to feed her, the bar was no place for a child. Agatka said, "It's no place for a husband either," and that's when she knocked her glass over and it shattered behind the counter. He came around the side of the bar, picked up the stroller with the child in it, and went down the stairs.

I tugged at the beginning of a hangnail. Agatka put her head down on the bar and closed her eyes. I wanted to lay my hand on her back, on her arm, but I didn't.

Ewa laid her cue stick across the table with relaxed ease, sauntered over in her broad-shouldered, slim-hipped way. Trobek took over behind the bar until the Arab returned and whispered, "Come, Agatka," and gently led her, hunched and weaving, down the stairs. A few middle-aged men came in, then some travelers with their suitcases, waiting for the late train to Rzeszów. When the Arab returned, he resumed pouring drinks, talking, joking with the customers as if nothing had happened. I was certain that when he started washing glasses and wiping down the counter, Ewa and I would get up to leave. I would say goodbye to the Arab the customary way: a light peck on both cheeks, a promise to visit again, an open, impossible invitation for him and Agatka to visit California—who could afford it? But after the other customers left, the Arab locked the door and put my mixtape in the boom box.

He put his arms around me, pulling me close enough that our hips bumped. I scooted back—I didn't want to feel anything else. He rested his chin on my shoulder, and I closed my eyes. I smelled his sweat, but saw lime and kelly green swirls on the back of my eyelids. I pulled away. "Ewa's turn," I said.

Ewa and the Arab waltzed around the pool table, singing loudly and drunkenly, nearly a foot's distance between them. Only their hands touched. Then Ewa grabbed me, waltzed me around the pool table, spun me back to the Arab, who dipped me and spun me to Trobek, and then it was just Trobek and me. We were alone in the corner, on the other side of the pool table, Ewa and the Arab together again, waltzing around and around, laughing. I tried not to want to be in Ewa's place.

Then I felt something warm and wet slide down my cheek, then my neck—Trobek, licking my jawbone, breathing hard, eyes closed. I pulled back and looked at him. His eyes were still closed, and his long lashes rested above those pitted cheeks. He put his hands on my face and pulled my head toward his. I had expected heat, but his tongue was a cool, motionless lump in my mouth. I thought of snails. I tasted pickles and kielbasa, vodka and cigarettes.

"Let's go down to the train station. I know a place," he said. He pawed at my crotch. I saw in my mind a dark alley, a pants zipper, fumbling, hands pushing at me, my hands pushing away.

"I don't want—I don't want—how do you say—?" The only word I could think of just then was the one Ewa had taught me: *stosunek*—one-night stand. I looked across the room. Ewa and the

Arab were still dancing. He was singing along to the music, mouthing English words he didn't understand but had memorized.

The Arab saw me. He cocked his head slightly to one side and said something to Ewa with a smile. She looked over at me and smiled too. She looked back at the Arab, and I saw her lips move. Then they both turned to look at me. They were both laughing. I shook my head, one quick sharp shake. The Arab motioned with his hand the way you'd wave to indicate a hesitant pedestrian should cross in front of your car at a stop sign.

I turned back to Trobek. "*Stosunek*," I said. "*Nie chce stosunka.*" Then I kissed one cheek, then the other and told him he always had a place to stay in California. I crossed the bar and did the same to the Arab—kiss-kiss, *zapraszamy do Californi!*

On our long, late walk home, I could tell it was the latest Ewa and I had ever stayed out. Dawn cracked the sky open directly ahead of us. I saw a narrow ribbon of purple-tinged gold at the horizon. I inhaled that wet, tilled-earth smell. My last night, my last morning. I asked Ewa if she'd seen Trobek kiss me.

"Did he try to take you to the train station?" Ewa asked.

"I told him I didn't want a one-night stand."

Ewa stopped walking, grabbed my arm, and pulled me to a stop, too. She was laughing so hard it took her a while to catch her breath. "What's so funny?" I asked again and again, and Ewa just shook her head. Finally, she dug into her purse for a cigarette, lit it, hooked arms with me once again and kept walking, waving her cigarette off to the side.

"So much to learn, so much to learn, *kuzynko.*" She looked up at the night sky with a smile. She seemed a million years older than I'd ever be.

She told me something else on that long, early-morning walk. Something wise, something about kisses being only kisses, that they didn't mean a thing. But I can't remember it exactly. I remember the walk, and her cigarette; I remember roosters crowing and the air being cool enough to make me stuff my hands into the pockets of my denim jacket, where I could feel the edge of the cassette a boy had given me half a world away. And I remember the dogs: three of them, small, barking and snapping, almost tripping over each other as they raced down the road toward us. Ewa scooped rocks from the edge of the road and threw them at the dogs. "*Do licha z wamy!*" Ewa yelled. To hell with you all. I stooped for rocks and threw them as far as I could.

Tenants

My friend Lila lives in my parents' house, in the suicide room, though she does not know that. It is the big, sunny bedroom above the kitchen, where she has hung purple batik across the windows and keeps a lizard named Malcolm in a glass-walled tank filled with driftwood. There are four bedrooms upstairs, but Lila chose this one. It faces east towards the bay and the Oakland Hills and is too bright to sleep in after sunrise, even with the shades pulled down. This, Lila says, is not the problem.

Lila is not like my other friends, my scientist friends. She is a massage therapist, a doula apprentice, and a self-proclaimed clairvoyant. She does less massage now that she's apprenticing and needs cheap rent. My parents' house has been empty for years. They live across town in a nursing home, but my mother isn't ready to sell.

When my mother and father actually lived here, when I'd come to visit, for my mother's sake, I'd stand in the street for a moment before going in, look up at the white stucco, green trim, two stories, and I'd imagine a giant wrecking ball—wide and silver and glinting—swinging into the side of the house—once, twice. Stucco and plaster and splintered wood flying everywhere. Upon impact, my mother would be down the block, dropping a letter in the mailbox.

Lila likes the house, and having her there is good for everyone. She gets a deal on the rent, and the house looks lived in. She brings in the mail, mows the lawn every other week, and talks to the plants. And since she's there, I haven't had to go over so often. Except when she asks me to.

Lila wants to give me a free massage as thanks for finding her cheap rent. I don't like massage—at least not from people I know— so she insists on cooking me dinner instead. You won't believe my curry, she says. Just you wait. When I come over, Lila is naked, cooking lentils in my mother's kitchen. Naan snaps and crackles in the oil of the frying pan. Lila says she believes in nudity the way she believes in democracy. If we all did it, it'd be the norm.

"Something weird happened last night," she says. I notice her breasts, long and droopy for someone in her mid-twenties, but with upturned nipples. I try not to stare. I don't think anyone has ever been naked in this kitchen.

"I was lying on my bed, reading, listening to music, and all of a sudden the volume shot up so loud I had to cover my ears and run to the stereo."

"What were you listening to?"

"Some people would say that's a sign of a poltergeist."

"Old house. Funky wiring."

"Weird," she says. "Just weird."

Until my father got sick and my parents moved to the nursing home, they slept in the dining room on separate beds in front of each of the china cabinets. Until I was ten, I slept in the trundle of my mother's bed, pulled out and filling the floor between the twin beds every night. Eventually my mother convinced my father that I needed my own bed and my own room, and they put me in the little den adjacent to the dining room, which my father had previously used as an office, scribbling out tenants' receipts at his huge oak desk.

Upstairs, in the four rooms designed for sleeping, we had tenants. The summer I was five, we had Don the Barber. He cut hair at the Command Performance Salon downtown. His own hair was shoulder-length and lustrous and gray and curly, and he had startling light blue eyes. He offered my mother a free haircut not long after he'd moved in—a welcome change from the severe, blunt bob she got from my father every other month. She accepted Don the Barber's offer—shyly—and when she came back with a soft, buoyant perm, my father took out his shears. He wanted to do a touch-up. My mother wore her bread-baking bandanna around her head for weeks after that, even when she slept.

In the west rooms, we had a Stanford law student named Rick and a man from Los Angeles who only stayed one or two nights a week, when he had business in San Francisco. In the northeast corner, we had Mr. King, who was old and small and hunchbacked. He looked like somebody's grandfather: grizzled and gray with sad eyes and hangdog jowls. I think he might have been a janitor somewhere. He always said hello to my mother in the yard, but he never looked up, never met her eyes. Once, when my mother heard him coughing for a few days upstairs, she took him some soup and fresh bread. After that, he took our broom out of the garage and swept our porch every day when he got home from work. Sometimes he sat in his car for a long time, parked on the street, and mumbled up at the closed sunroof. I was eating peanut butter cookies at the table when he shot himself with a rifle in the room above our kitchen.

Lila calls me at work.

"I felt something last night," she says.

"What's his name?"

"Shut up. It was a presence. I was lying in bed—shut up—and I felt something fluttering around my ear, like a moth. But I knew it wasn't. And then I knew right away what it was."

"And?"

"I told it to go away. In a firm voice. I told it to leave me and not come back. And it left."

"You should get mothballs for the closet. There might be some downstairs. Check the armoires. In the dining room."

"Do you know you have a ghost?"

"Your rent isn't going to get cheaper."

"We need an exorcism."

"You said it went away."

"It'll be back. You should have seen the way Malcolm was trying to climb out of his tank."

"Call me when the exorcism is over."

"It's your house," she says. "Only you can make him leave."

"Technically, it's my father's house. Maybe we should bring him down from the nursing home for the day," I say. "Sorry—experiment's running. Gotta go."

My mother had to unlock Mr. King's door with our landlord key. I remember her whole body shook. I held onto to her knees, peered between her legs. She said, "Holy Mary, Mother of God," over and over. Don, who worked evenings at the salon, stood in the hallway. When my mother opened the door, I saw red-splattered wall and then nothing, because she'd thrust my face against her pant leg. Don grabbed her shoulders, turned her away. My father came home from work early, swinging two cans of semi-gloss in pale pistachio. It was what he'd painted all the tenants' rooms. Green didn't show dirt.

"Last night I saw him here." Lila stands at the bottom of the staircase, ankle deep in forest green shag. "At the top. Like a kid on a porch step waiting for someone to play with him. I was coming up the stairs, and just for a split second, I saw him. And then he was gone. He's afraid of me, that's why."

At the top of the staircase, Lila has arranged objects she found downstairs. "They need to be organic to the spirit's environment," she says. She has wrapped her dreadlocks up in a green silk scarf—I have never seen it before, so either it's new or it's her exorcism scarf or both. At the top step, she has clustered the framed photograph of Pope John Paul II, my mother's green, gold-edged porcelain tea set from the kitchen cupboard, a bar of soap, an acorn from the front lawn, and my father's cordless power drill.

I pick up the drill, turn it over in my hands. "Vatican II?" I ask.

She lights candles, one on each step. She has wrapped herself in one of the batiks from her windows. I am surprised she is not naked.

At the bottom of the staircase, she grabs my hand and hums for a minute.

"Tell him to leave this house, to join his spirit friends in his spirit home. This is an earth home. This is no longer his home."

"You should stick to massage. And midwifery."

"This isn't that different."

"I do science. Not ghosts. Or exorcisms."

"You'll never be free of him."

"How can I not be free of something I don't believe in?"

Silence. Lila stares at me, hard. "I've known you a long time but I don't know very much about you," she says. "I do know something weird happened in this house, and that is why you are the way you are. You hide behind gels and pipettes and sarcasm and grid-lined notebooks and you won't let anyone touch you—not a massage or a hug or even—"

She drops my hand. "He's here," she says. "Do you see him?"

"Where?"

"There."

I say, "No, Lila, I don't see anything at all. No ghosts."

It's only a partial lie. I don't see the kind of ghosts she's talking about.

I met Lila in a laundromat off Telegraph my senior year of college. She picked up a pair of underwear I'd dropped in transferring a load from washer to dryer, held them out to me, dangling the damp white cotton off her index finger, nails painted bright blue.

"Boring," she said. I looked at her, then at my underwear.

"No," she said. "In here. No one to talk to." She picked up her purse—a colorful, woven, Guatemalan thing—and took out a deck of tarot cards.

"I'll give you a reading," she said. "Free. I'm practicing."

I was supposed to be studying for my genetics midterm, but Lila hopped up on the sorting table, sat down cross-legged, and fanned out the cards. It wasn't the sort of thing I found the least bit interesting. I never even read my horoscope. But when Lila said, "Choose one," I did, sliding the card out facedown as she instructed. And while she arranged other cards around it, began turning them over, I thought, maybe she can tell me who I am.

She squinted at the cards, referred to her manual, tucked between her thigh and the tabletop. She tapped a finger against her pursed lips, looked up at me occasionally. Finally, she swept the cards with one hand, mussed them into a giant pile.

"You," she said, "are someone who needs a someone like me."

For awhile after I was born, my father slept upstairs and my mother and I slept downstairs. He couldn't sleep if I woke up and cried in the night. He kept that room vacant for years, the smallest room in the northwest corner—too small to really rent out. He would lock himself in and turn up his radio. Once, when I was sick and my mother needed to go to the pharmacy, she had to call a neighbor because my father wouldn't come out of his room to take her. He couldn't hear her over the Bing Crosby.

After my father was laid off and they needed the money from that room, too, he came back downstairs. I was older then, and I didn't cry so much. But sometimes, in the middle of the night, my mattress dipped under the weight of my mother's foot, and I heard the door to the upstairs open, then close. Sometimes I followed her, pressed my ear to the door, and listened to her weeping on the bottom stair.

Lila did not grow up like I did. For years, she lived with her mother on a commune near Sebastopol, in fiberglass domes with blue mold on the walls. Every night a different dome family cooked, and on weekends, someone dug a pit and they filled a big, round cattle trough with water, heated it up, sliced carrots and onions, and jumped in naked. Cannibal pot, they called it. They had a pet chicken named Necky, and when it got sick, they had a meeting and voted to take Necky to the vet, even though it would cost money.

Money wasn't something they had a lot of at the domes, according to Lila. There were no lack of fathers, though. None of them was Lila's birth father, who, she'd been told, was a motorcycle mechanic living outside Topeka. Apart from that, all her mother would tell her was that he hadn't been particularly loving. And that was what Lila's mother came to the Russian River for—loving people. All of Lila's adoptive fathers were very loving. Lila told me that it took years and a school counselor to figure out that some of them were too loving. She hasn't talked to her mother since she dropped out of high school and moved in with her aunt in Denver.

Now Lila lives only two hours away from the domes, and knows from her aunt that her mother still lives there, but she has never gone back to visit. Sometimes I want to go in her place. I don't know why.

Even after my parents no longer kept tenants, after I was sent to college and my education was paid for, my parents continued to sleep in the dining room—a swinging door from the kitchen, two double french doors out onto the patio. My father's machinist handbooks in one china cabinet, my mother's volumes of *Stories of the Saints* in the cabinet that used to hold my stuffed animals. A threadbare, imitation Oriental carpet lay between the two twin beds. Two armoires in the corners. A painting of Jesus above my father's bed, a photograph of the Pope above my mother's.

My parents slept in that room for thirty-four years, until my father could no longer remember his name or my mother's or mine, and when he had to go to the nursing home, my mother went with him. At first, she tried to go just for the daytime, and she'd come home at night, but she was scared, all alone in that big house. She called me to come stay with her, and she turned back the covers on my father's empty bed. For almost a year, a few nights a week, I'd sleep in my father's bed while my mother snored lightly across the room. She woke up at six o'clock every morning, before her alarm. "Oh, *jej*," she gasped. "Time to get up. Don't be late." She'd been responsible for getting my father to work on time all those years. She only overslept once that I know of, and it never happened again.

More and more, my mother didn't want to leave my father alone at the nursing home for the nights. She started sleeping in a chair next to his bed, and then the nurses got her a cot, and she slept on that for a few months. Finally, the nursing home staff found a double room, and now, although there's nothing physically wrong with my mother, she lives in the nursing home, too.

74

When I visit, I must visit the both of them. I never stay for long. When I leave, I say goodbye to my father, who blinks at me. And I pat my mother on the shoulder. When I was little, she trained me to hug her only when my father wasn't in the room so he wouldn't get jealous. Now, at the end of my visits, she trails after me into the hallway in her pajamas and slippers and hugs me by the elevator.

My mother and I talk about renting the whole house out— not just a room upstairs for Lila, but the whole house, for a whole family. Eventually, we'll have to either rent or sell to pay for the nursing home. But if we rent, we'll have to change things around. Take out the furniture. Make the dining room the dining room again. My mother says I should do it anyway. For Lila. So she has somewhere to eat. Somewhere to invite guests. All alone in that big house, my mother says. She should have friends over.

She eats in the kitchen, I tell her. Just like we did.

Still, when my mother says this, I call Lila. It's been a week since the aborted exorcism and it's not like her to be sullen.

"I was worried the ghost got you."

"Ha," she says.

"My mother thinks you need a dining room."

"Downstairs?" she says. "I don't usually eat there. I eat in my room. The downstairs has a dark energy."

"Just you and the ghost upstairs, though."

"He's not harmful," she says.

"Then why are you trying to get rid of him?"

"Maybe I'm not anymore. Maybe we keep each other company."

The day after I call her, Lila calls me. Dinner, she says. Apology. "I always say, if you've got something to say, say it with food."

"I like your Thai," I tell her.

"I'll wear it just for you."

"Ha." I say. "Ha. Ha."

When I come into the kitchen, calling Lila's name, she glides out of my parents' "bedroom," the door swinging gently behind her.

I raise my eyebrows. "Taking a nap?"

"Re-hanging the Pope."

The kitchen smells of coconut milk and steamed rice. Empty cans and vegetable trimmings coat the counters. On the kitchen table, overturned spice jars are surrounded by little spilled heaps like mine tailings. Malcolm sits in the middle of the floor, motionless until I step over him. He darts under the table.

Lila lifts a platter of dishes high in one hand, like a maître'd'. She looks at me and says, "Let me show you to your table." She pushes through the swinging door and flicks the light switch in my parents' bedroom.

The beds are gone. The armoires are gone. My mother's gold-edged tea set has been placed throughout the china cabinets—a cup or two per shelf. The drapes—thick and red and heavy—are gone. The doors are open—all of them—to the living room, the den, the patio. It is dark and cold outside and a breeze blows in, threatens to extinguish the candles on the card table in the middle of the room. Only the rug remains. The rug and the Pope and Jesus.

Lila places the platter on the table, pulls out a folding chair for me.

"Exorcism II," she says.

I sit down but I do not lift my napkin. I leave my hands folded in my lap. "Where's everything? How did you get it out of here?"

She smiles. "I got some help. I told you he wasn't harmful." She pauses. "I'm sensing things." She lifts her arms, palms upward. The folds of her crocheted purple poncho hang straight down from her arms, like vestments. "You slept in this room, didn't you?"

"It's not a secret. My mother told you?"

"You slept in this room until you were ten, in a trundle between your mother and your father. And then you moved into the den."

"I can't deny any of it." I pick up my fork.

"What happened to you here? What happened in this room?"

"I slept. I sliced open my stuffed animals and tried to sew them back together. I did whatever kids do in their rooms."

"Except you did it with your parents."

I lay down my fork. "What are you asking me?"

"What do you want to tell me?"

"In what way is this an apology?"

Lila looks at me so hard I want to turn around, look over my shoulder.

"I see," she says, "a woman who can't mention her father without her whole body tensing. I see a woman who wears clothes two sizes too big for her. I see a woman who jumps when I touch her."

"I see a woman who sees what's not there."

"Exactly."

I have never thrown anything out of passion in my life, but that fork flies out the open patio doors and clatters onto the flagstones. And I want more. I want cups, plates, glass, my mother's gold-edged tea set. I want to throw it all.

"That's a start," Lila says.

"Why do you want to know what happened? Why do you care?"

Lila folds her arms across her chest, lifts her chin.

"All right." I shrug. "But you're going to be disappointed. Yes, I slept in here with my parents. Twice, maybe three times, my father stepped across me to climb in bed with my mother to warm his feet. And then he stepped back across me. I have never seen my parents kiss. I have never even seen them hug. I would bet my life on there not being sex after me. I wish I could tell you what you want to hear."

"And what about upstairs?"

"Him? Don't you already know?"

"Not him. After."

My mother scrubbed the blood all evening. She dipped the hard-bristled brush in a bucket of ammonia, while my father ate pork chops and sauerkraut at the kitchen table. She came downstairs to make him a cup of tea—he'd never made one for himself—and she turned on the TV for him while he put his feet up on the coffee table. Then she went back upstairs to paint. She painted that same night so the room could be advertised the next day. I didn't have to sleep in the trundle that night, because she never came to bed. I crept up the stairs, and at the top, I rested my chin on the banister. On the other side of the wall, I heard the slap of the brush against the plaster and my mother crying. A strip of light appeared under Don the Barber's door, and then I heard bedsprings and floorboards and I turned and went down the stairs. From the darkness at the bottom, I watched him cross the hall, and I heard murmurings and mumblings and then my mother's voice a little louder, a little firmer, then a shushing noise. "Please," I heard my mother say. "Don't."

And then Don the Barber walked back across the hall, shut the door. His light didn't go off, but I went to bed anyway. I woke up at six o'clock when my mother came downstairs and made my father breakfast and packed his lunch and carried it out to his car and went down to the Tribune to place a new ad: Room for rent. Just painted. Please inquire.

In the afternoon, she painted a second coat, and then you almost couldn't see the stains.

I stand above my plate, stare down at Lila, a spoon in my hand. I step around the table, my thigh knocking it forward so Lila's plate jolts toward her. She catches it before it lands in her lap. Then I am outside, on the patio, breathing cold air and looking up at the house, arms wrapped around my sides. Light shines in Lila's windows upstairs.

I feel her standing next to me, can hear her breathe. I smell her—patchouli and cooking oil and unwashed hair and, beneath it all, beneath it all, Ivory soap.

She drapes her purple poncho around me without touching me. It settles on my shoulders like dust.

When she goes back inside, she closes the glass doors behind her—just shuts them, leaving one slightly open, the lock tab resting against the other door's edge. When she turns in the light of the chandelier to clear the table, I see that she hasn't been wearing anything at all under that poncho. Not even a bra.

I wish my mother had let Don the Barber help her paint that room. I wish she had locked the door behind him, pressed herself against him, and cried into chest, his shoulders, his long gray hair. I wish she had undressed him, or he had undressed her. I wish they'd made love quietly on top of drop cloths, among ladders and paint cans and newspapers and wet brushes. I wish for once, just once, my mother had felt something like pleasure, something like love.

***

It is past midnight when I buzz the fourth floor nurse's desk from the sliding glass doors of the main entrance. I lift a hand to wave at the camera, and the doors open. Visiting hours have long since ended, but the nurses know me here. They are accustomed to me, to my parents' "special" situation.

They are perhaps not as accustomed to seeing me at midnight in a purple poncho, spoon in hand. But at the same time, night nurses see many things. Weirder things. I push open the door into my parents' room without a single person stopping me.

What I see is what I've never seen before: My parents sleep in two separate hospital beds, yes, but my mother's bed is pushed all the way over to my father's side of the room, snug against his. My father's bed tilts ergonomically so that he almost sits straight up. My mother's mattress is horizontal. She sleeps on her side, one arm flung over the railing of my father's bed, her hand in his. The bathroom light is on—a nightlight of sorts—and I step closer. My father opens his eyes, looks at me, blinks, then goes back to sleep.

I inspect the hands. Both are wrinkled, the skin loose and liver-spotted, my father's nails too long, my mother's bitten close. I try to see if my father's hand grips tight, or if my mother's is twisted into his in any way. But all I see are the hands of two people sleeping, hands enfolded in one another, relaxed, loose, lightly touching.

George Foreman Grill, George Foreman Grill

Every evening at my mother's house, while I tamp down the lids of the paint cans and rinse the brushes, my fiancé grills on the George Foreman. He grills salmon steaks, kielbasa, chicken breasts, eggplant, even asparagus and thin strips of red pepper. Then he sets the table under the apricot tree. All week long, we sit down to heaps of food, to cloth napkins he's unearthed from a drawer, to wine glasses from the shelf my mother can't reach.

On our last night, Jay makes teriyaki pork chops, warm potato salad, and green beans. He pours the wine and tells us he's having a love affair with meat. Suddenly, grilling is so easy, he says. None of that Hibachi business, the coals, the lighter fluid. My mother eats slowly and shyly. She looks up into the amber light peculiar to California; it slants through the leaves.

"So nice to be cooked for," she says. "Everything tastes better." She turns to me. "You lucky." She's been saying it all week because Jay is kind and funny and cooks for me and is not like my father. When he was alive, he expected my mother to remove his shoes and socks the instant he got home from work and then to shuttle hot dishes from stove to table. My mother and I ate together afterward. When I left for college, she ate in the den where I used to sleep while my father read the newspaper in bed. Now she eats alone.

Every night after dinner, my mother tells us how grateful she is that we've come to repaint the house. It was Jay's idea. Last summer, when we visited for the first time together, he asked my mother what she wanted us to do—repairs, improvements, that kind of thing. Oh, nothing, she said, just relax. Have a good time. Let me look at you two, that's all.

This summer we're painting all the downstairs rooms Hushed White. My father believed white was the only proper color for a wall, and my mother wants the same thing. Just a fresh coat, she says.

Every afternoon, she sits on a folding chair and tells us she'd have painted it herself if not for her varicose veins; they make it hard to stand for very long. Then she tells us to take whatever we want, whatever we see, it's all ours. All week long, she's been telling me to take the George Foreman grill. Jay likes it so much, she says. And all week long, I refuse. This is how it always is. If she sees I like something, she tries to give it to me. And even if I want it, I decline. Now, over our last dinner, she tries again.

"Take the grill," she says. "Take it. I don't need it. I never use it."

I tell her we don't need one.

I tell her we don't have room. In the car. In our kitchen back in Utah.

I tell her we need it here for when we visit.

"Take it, take it," she says.

I turn to Jay. "Don't we already have one, tucked away somewhere? See, we don't even know. We never use it."

"Don't tease," my mother says. She means: don't lie.

Jay and I have made a joke of the George Foreman in bed. Right before we fall asleep, or first thing in the morning, our legs tangled under sheets, one of us clamps both thighs around the other's and makes a sizzling sound, like meat on a grill. We whisper, "George Foreman grill! George Foreman grill!" We think it's hilarious but try to stifle our laughter; my mother sleeps next door.

Our first night here, after that long drive, we were too tired to do anything but roll toward each other before we fell asleep. But the next night, after grilling my thigh, Jay flipped on top of me and pinned me down with one of his legs pressed between mine, his breath warm and close on my neck. "George Foreman grill, George Foreman grill," he whispered again, differently this time. I could smell

81

the paint flecked through his hair.

"Not here," I whispered.

"Aw, c'mon, babe," he said, between kisses along my jaw. "We do it at my parents' house."

"Yeah, because we stay above the garage, not in the room next door." I pushed him off, just slightly, and he rolled the rest of the way on his own. Now Jay goes straight to sleep every night after we play George Foreman grill, and the last couple of nights we haven't played at all. I still haven't told him that my mother doesn't sleep lightly, and these walls aren't thin.

After our last dinner, Jay cleans the grill and places it in the cupboard, then washes the rest of the dishes. My mother protests—you cooked! You're tired!—but lets him. While I wipe the counters, she pulls the grill out of the cupboard and puts it in the pile with everything else she insists we take back with us, including a huge bag of oranges. No matter how many times I've told her, she doesn't believe you can buy citrus in Utah. Oranges just don't grow there, I tell her, but you can get them in the stores.

I pluck the grill off the bag of oranges and put it back in the cupboard. My mother picks up a dishtowel and dries the plates. I take out the trash, and when I return, an electrical cord pokes out from among the oranges. I dump them on the table and remove the grill.

"Ah, my legs," my mother says. She collapses into a chair and massages one of her calves. With her other hand, she flaps her dishtowel at me. "You!" she says. "So stubborn." Jay looks up from the sudsy dishpan and smiles.

I step over and tap my finger against his breastbone. "I am not stubborn," I say.

Upstairs in the bathroom, we brush our teeth. While I begin counting one, one thousand all the way to sixty in my head, and then over again, for a full two minutes, Jay says, "Maybe it's easier just to take the thing?"

I poke him in the ribs, harder than I mean to. "Whose side are you on anyway?"

Jay spits and cups his hands to rinse. He presses the towel to his mouth, then holds up one finger. "First, ow," he says. "Second," he lifts both hands and shrugs, "I'm on the side of the meat."

Jay goes to our room, and I start over with the counting because I can't remember where I stopped. Then I take my diamond ring off the windowsill, where I lay it every morning so I don't get

Hushed White on it, and I climb into bed. Jay lies on his side, facing me, already almost asleep. I nestle my backside against his front, and he drapes an arm and a leg over me. He's wedged against me the way I love, his chest a warm wall at my back, his hand on my belly. I slide my arm out from under his and touch the cool, stippled wall above the wooden headboard. We'll paint this wall next summer.

I whisper over my shoulder to Jay, "You know I was just kidding, right? About sides?" I slide my arm under the covers.

"Sure, babe," he says, and I nestle into him even more. Then he thrusts his lower leg between mine and squeezes. He whispers, "George Foreman grill! George Foreman grill!" I try to laugh, but I can't. Jay's thighs ease their grip.

"It's okay," he says. "I thought it might get old." He kisses the back of my head, yawns into my hair, and wiggles a little to settle in for sleep. I want to reassure him: it is still funny. I can't explain why I'm not laughing and why, suddenly, I could cry if I let myself. I reach up to touch the cool wall again. It feels chalky beneath my fingertips. Next year we'll paint the other side, too, where my mother sleeps. Maybe we can convince her to use a color: Honey Butter or Peach Fade. Something warmer.

Then I slide my hand to the smooth, polished edge of the wooden headboard. I bump my hips back a little, jostling Jay slightly in his sleep. He groans but doesn't move. I nudge him one more time. He stirs and says, "What's wrong?"

"Nothing," I whisper.

"Then why are you waking me up?" I don't answer; I just nudge him again. He's still for a moment, alert. He rolls over me as I roll under him. We're moving so quietly that the sheets hardly rustle, but Jay whispers, "You sure?"

I reach my legs around him, dig my heels into his calves, squeeze his hips with my thighs to wedge him closer. I curl my fingers over the headboard. The wooden edge digs into my wrists, but I don't let go. The joints of the old bed creak and Jay checks again: "Okay?"

"Don't worry," I whisper. "Really." The wheels start to rattle off the wagon—Jay calls it that—and soon our breath is ragged and raspy in each other's ears.

We stay clamped together a while, quiet, just drifting back from outer space, and then he slides off me and cuddles against me, and soon I hear his measured breathing. Sleep for him, but I lie awake. I touch the wall again, and I hear my mother snoring faintly in her bed.

I imagine her in the morning, as we drive off. I'll glance in the rearview mirror and see her waving goodbye in the driveway, flapping her dishtowel. The worry will show in the furl of her brows—did we eat enough, did we get enough sleep, do we have enough money for gas? Maybe we should stay another day, get another night's rest. The electrical cord will snake out from the trunk, trailing on the pavement behind our car. I'll see that in the rearview mirror, too. We'll pull over a few blocks away, and I'll tell Jay we should leave the grill on the curb or some neighbor's porch. I'll mock-strangle myself with the cord, but then I'll stuff the cord beneath duffel bags and sacks of oranges, secure the trunk, and get back on the road. Jay will look at me, curious, but I'll look straight ahead. I'll concentrate on driving.

By nightfall, Jay and I will roll into Salt Lake, bleary-eyed and a little sour-smelling, too tired to shower. We'll drop into bed, tease each other about how stinky we are, reach for each other's warm haunches anyway, and probably fall asleep mid-kiss, exhausted but happy, as happy as I'll ever be when thinking of my mother, eight hundred miles behind us, climbing into a bed where, as always, any warmth is all her own.

The Painting

When the noon bell rang at the coat factory, my mother
punched her timecard and walked directly to the train station. She
loved to go to Kraków alone on Saturdays. All afternoon she walked
the cobblestone streets that spilled onto the pigeon-infested squares,
and sometimes she bought pastries to snack on—crispy wafer tubes
filled with cream, or sugar-glazed buns. Sometimes she stepped into
the cathedral on Plac Kosciuszko and sat in a back pew, relishing
the dim, echoing quiet—so beautiful after the relentless thrum of
the machines in the sewing hall. Mostly she window-shopped and
dreamed of a new dresser—something dark, mahogany maybe, or
black walnut, and a real dining table set so she could invite Goszka
and the other girls from the factory over for dinner parties. But if
she bought anything, it was usually something small—a spatula for
the kitchen or a doily for the coffee table. They were things she could
have bought at home in Trzebinia, but purchasing them in Kraków
made them seem special, like souvenirs.

On this particular Saturday, she stopped in front of the
window of an art gallery on Florianska Street. A painting had caught
her attention. The sun glowed deep red in one corner of the canvas,
and radiated orange and yellow light across a marsh. Reeds bowed

and waved in a breeze; dark trees stood at the left edge of the canvas. But the reeds weren't green the way she expected reeds to be—they were splashed in the apricot light of the sun. Yes, that was exactly as they would look, with light on them. She stood in front of it—she didn't know how long—trying to figure out if the sun was rising or setting over the marsh. It was about the size of the upper third of a door; she measured it with her eyes, thinking already of which wall it would fit on.

She walked in, the bell jangling as the door swung shut behind her. She turned to the shopkeeper—a balding man slumped behind the counter, smoking a cigarette, the pages of the *Tygodnik* spread out in front of him.

"Excuse me, sir. How much for this painting?"

He glanced up, then back down at the newspaper.

"A thousand zloty," he said without looking at her. A month's pay. She had two hundred—maybe two hundred fifty—zloty in her purse, and another hundred in an empty coffee canister in her kitchen, but it still wouldn't be enough. She didn't even bother asking if she could put the painting on layaway. The store was state-run; the man behind the counter would get paid whether the paintings sat on the walls or not. My mother looked around at the other canvases—mountains and forests, cityscapes, farmland—but her eyes always fell back to the marsh. She stood in front of it until she was embarrassed that she had been in the shop so long. The bell on the door jangled once more as she walked out, and she blinked in the brightness of the street. She was not seeing the sun over the shops and the street and the cars. In her eyes, the sun still poured molten gold over reeds and dark trees.

On Sunday morning, while she boiled water for her after-church tea and sliced bread and butter, she glanced out her little kitchen window, and far below, in the sprawling backyard of her apartment building, she saw her landlady's son with his thinning, grayish hair. He held a cigarette in one hand—his mother wouldn't let him smoke in the house—and a bouquet of pink and purple flowers in the other.

The house had once belonged to a farm on the outskirts of Trzebinia, but now the town spread all around them, and parcels of land had been chopped off, one by one, for tall, dismal concrete housing. But Zielinski's backyard, ringed in alder and birch, was like a little piece of the open countryside, and in the spring, he grew tulips, row after row of them, and chrysanthemums in the fall. On Saturdays, he sold bouquets at a table he set up in front of the house.

My mother had a hunch the flowers would be for her. He often brought her flowers on weekends, saying they were from his mother, that his mother had told him to pick them, that she would have picked them herself if she could bend over that far. But she knew it was an excuse to check up on her in a friendly way. She knew there was nothing romantic in the gift of flowers; Zielinski had a sort of fatherliness, although he had no children and had never married. He was in his mid-forties and still lived with his ailing mother.

My mother felt sorry for him; every evening he rode his moped down the block and turned left at the corner to visit a woman who lived on Ulica Jablonska. Her name was Tosza, and my mother had seen her once, riding on the back of the moped when they passed by the house. She had copper hair in a startling, unnatural shade. It flowed behind her, most of it protected beneath a scarf tied around her head. She'd wrapped her bare arms tightly around Zielinski's waist, and her skin was pale against his brown leather jacket. Zielinski had not even looked up at the house, as if he were riding through a new neighborhood and no house was any more significant than any other. A neighbor had once whispered to my mother that Zielinski had been courting Tosza for twenty years now but his mother forbade him from marrying her. Tosza's older sister had divorced her husband—a disgrace to the entire family. The neighbor had said that Zielinski was just waiting for the old woman to die.

My mother didn't believe her. She could see that Zielinski loved his mother. He called her *mamusiu*, as a little boy would, and cooked for her every day when he got home from his job as a clerk at the courthouse. Passing by the open door to Zielinski's apartment, my mother often saw him carrying a carefully loaded dinner tray, complete with a vase of flowers from the garden, into the old woman's bedroom. On their evening walks, Zielinski kept one arm around the old woman's thick waist and one hand under her elbow, supporting her as she hobbled.

But once, nearly a year earlier, on a Saturday evening, my mother had come up the stone walkway after spending the afternoon in Kraków, and had heard the old woman shouting, "Stasiu! *Pomocy!*" My mother dropped her satchel in the front hall and burst through the old woman's door. Pani Zielinski lay on the kitchen floor. My mother tried to lift her but only succeeded in dragging her a few inches. "Find Stasiu," the woman cried. Zielinski had gone to a nephew's wedding in Katowice, she said, and should have been back already.

My mother ran out to check the yard. "Pan Zielinski, Pan Zielinski," she called, and then she saw him, about halfway down the stretch of the yard, at the edge of the chrysanthemum field. He crouched on his heels, his back against an alder trunk. He wore a suit and tie and shiny black shoes, and he was smoking. In one hand, he held a pale pink rosebud, his boutonniere. He twirled it around and around between his fingers. Standing above him, panting slightly from the sprint, my mother said, "The old lady fell in the kitchen."

Zielinski looked up. "I'm coming," he said. He pushed himself off the trunk and jogged up the path. The cigarette and rosebud lay at my mother's feet. From where she stood, she could hear Pani Zielinski calling her son's name.

Within weeks, my mother forgot that moment, perhaps because she wanted to. She lost herself in her own life and work. She was grateful that no one told her with whom she could or couldn't go to the theater or out for coffee. A handful of young men courted her—Bogdan, who worked in the bookshop, and Piotrek, the butcher's son, studying to be a teacher. She didn't like any of them enough to marry, but she liked letting them grasp her hand in dark movie theaters and having them over for tea.

She added more water to the little pot boiling on her stove, and when she heard footsteps on the attic stairs, she knew they were Zielinski's boots. Her door was ajar and he poked his head and chest inside, nearly sideways, the rest of his body still hidden by the wall. He thrust the fistful of flowers toward her.

"Beautiful!" she said. She brought the bouquet to her nose and closed her eyes. Phlox was her favorite flower. A large bush of it grew by her mother's garden gate. "Pan Zielinski, where are these from?"

"The Komarskis across the street."

"Pan Zielinski! Did you poach these? Tell the truth." My mother was laughing. She inverted the bouquet so that the blooms faced the floor. If you did that for a minute, she believed, gravity would help keep the plant juices flowing toward the flowers; they'd live longer.

"You know the saying, what's theirs is mine and what's mine is mine, too," Zielinski said. "Are you keeping warm enough up here?"

My mother's apartment had once been old Pan Zielinski's woodcarving shop. It had never been properly heated; in the evenings when the cold set in, he had simply escaped to the lower floors. My mother had only a pot-bellied coal stove in the partitioned kitchen behind the curtain. It was big enough to hold one pot at a time so that she could not make tea at the same time she cooked soup or boiled sausages, and it did not heat the apartment sufficiently in the coldest months.

Despite this nuisance, my mother loved her apartment. Her heaven, she called it. She had grown up in a two-room farmhouse in Zarębki with five brothers and sisters and a roof of thatched straw, and nothing had ever been her own. Sometimes at dusk when she was out far enough in the pasture with the two old black cows she tended and the crowded house was distant, she turned her back on it and pretended it was not there. She pretended everything she could see in front of her was her own. She was the queen of the fields and the forests and all the neighbors' houses.

Zielinski had been kind enough to repaint her apartment the way she'd always dreamed. She'd seen it in a book about castles: walls covered with pale blue wallpaper, embossed with a silver pattern, stripes of curling leaves. But wallpaper was expensive, so Zielinski covered the white walls with blue paint—like the sky over Zarębki at dusk, and my mother stenciled the silver leaves in a pattern of stripes.

Eventually she added a faded, second-hand Oriental rug; a huge, highly polished dark wooden armoire with oval-mirrored doors (she had worked extra shifts, sewing coats late into the night for that); and a *tapczan* that folded out for a bed. She had a record player and box of records—mostly big band orchestras and folk melodies—and two little wooden tables with intricately embroidered doilies on which she now set her china cups and teapot.

"What new riches did Pani Julka bring home to her castle today?" Zielinski asked, his hands in his pockets. He looked around the little room, smiling.

She motioned for him to sit on the *tapczan*. She sat on the chair across from him and told him about the beautiful painting on Florianska Street. She described it in detail, closing her eyes and pressing her hands together over her heart. "It was the most beautiful thing I've ever seen," she said. "Do you like paintings?"

"I get restless looking at paintings," he said. "I would rather stand in an open field, with dirt under my feet, than in front of a wall."

"I come from the countryside, too. I understand. But I think this painting may have been more beautiful than any countryside I've ever seen."

"Why didn't you buy it?"

She looked down and stirred her tea with the little silver-plated spoon. "I'm going to save up for it."

"That's good," he said. "It's good to wait for what you want." Zielinski looked into his own tea and stirred it. Then he said, "Florianska Street? Isn't that near the old marketplace? They have beautiful things there," he said. "A leather belt or a new coat. Now that's something worth spending money on."

Old Mrs. Zielinski's voice drifted up from below. "Stasiu?" Zielinski laid his spoon on the saucer, spread his hands out, palms up, glanced at my mother with a half-smile, and stood up.

My mother washed the teacups in her little sink and decided she wouldn't go to the movies with Goszka that night. No, she would eat broth and bread for the next two weeks, maybe some sausage and apples, but not much more. When she had saved up enough money, she would go to Kraków. Already she knew where she would hang her painting—on the silver and blue wall above the *tapczan*. She would go to sleep in the glow of the painting's sunset at night, and wake under its dawn every morning. Her guests would sit beneath it as they drank their tea. She could admire it as she talked to them. These were the thoughts that floated in the back of her mind as she stitched at her machine in the long workday hours, as she drifted off to sleep, as she said her prayers at night, kneeling beneath the expectant wall.

That week, when she passed Zielinski in the stairwell in the mornings outside the vine-covered garage and he said, "How is the lady art collector today?" my mother always laughed. One evening, she called hello to him from her kitchen window. He was in the backyard, weeding the chrysanthemums on his knees on a flat board to protect his pants from the mud.

"Have you brought home your painting yet, Pani Julka?" he called.

She called back, "Two more weeks!"

He stretched his arm out, a sweeping gesture indicating the rows of flowers—gold and copper and burgundy and yellow. "What do you need a painting for, Pani Julka? Here is your Van Gogh. Here

90

is your Monet."

The next Saturday after work, she walked straight home. She did not even buy buns. Usually it was hard for her to pass the bakery without popping in, but that day she walked purposefully, with her head high, gave a nod and a wave at the baker in his apron behind the glass case. No, she would not go to Kraków today, nor the next weekend. But the following one—then she would go, and she would buy her painting. She rounded the corner of her block.

Old Mrs. Zielinski sat at the flower stand, bundled up in blankets and shawls, a wool scarf knotted under her bristly chin, and a row of chrysanthemum bouquets in pickle jars in front of her. She grumbled to my mother that her son had gone off somewhere, had left her out there at the mercy of strangers—an old woman, sick, dying.

My mother hurried up the stairs. She was impatient to wipe down the blue and silver walls and capture the cobwebs in the corners. The following weekend she would scrub the floors and beat the rug in the backyard. Zielinski would help her carry it down. He would laugh and tease her, but he would do it. She wanted the apartment immaculate when her painting came home.

She had just placed her handbag on the table by the door and was opening the doors of the armoire to hang up her coat when, outside, someone revved a moped louder and louder. It sounded as if it were coming up the drive. She went to the window. Zielinski usually tended his chrysanthemums on Saturday afternoons and did not go out until Saturday evenings, when he rode down the street and turned left at the corner.

When she parted the lace panels between the two heavy blue velvet curtains, she saw Zielinski gunning his moped up the center of the street. He did not look up at the house, but stared directly ahead, one hand on the handlebars, the other hugging to his chest a brown rectangle wrapped in paper and string and approximately the size of the upper third of a door.

My mother let the lace panel sway between the outer curtains and turned away. Directly across from her gaped the bareness of the blue and silver wall, a bareness that had not been there before. In a few moments, she would remember Tosza's arms tight around Zielinski's jacketed waist, the boutonniere crushed to a pulp in the dirt of the backyard. But not yet. She placed one hand on her belly, pressed hard, and resolved at that moment to keep her desires to herself.

The Company She Keeps

Late last summer my fiancé's father built us a compost bin out of old railroad ties. We smelled the creosote as we shimmied the bin into place against the side fence. The bin had two compartments. First, we would fill up one side; then we would transfer the compost to the other side so that the bottom layers got exposed to air. The first things my fiancé and I dropped into our new compost bin were the remnants of our summer breakfasts: grapefruit rinds, coffee grounds, egg shells. Then it was fall, and we filled the bin with leaves. They sank surprisingly quickly, flattened by nothing other than gravity. We added drifts and drifts of leaves. Then it was winter: food scraps, snow, food scraps, snow.

Now it is June. Two days ago my fiancé came up behind me in the linen closet to tell me he began an affair with our friend Emily last September, not long after we installed the compost bin. The affair ended in January, when Emily began sleeping with our other friend, Gil. My fiancé and I have not yet postponed our wedding. In fact, we are deep in a frenzy of activity. Yesterday, his parents helped us lay a new patio. They did not know anything. A young, injured blue jay dragged itself around a corner of the backyard, so we kept the cat indoors. Today the blue jay is gone, and we weed the vegetable garden, turn the compost. The cat wanders purposefully among the plants.

We take turns transferring the compost with a pitchfork, pitching the layers over into the empty side, until we get to the leaves I dumped in there last fall. They cling together in shiny, putrid drifts and emit a terrible smell, a shit smell, not like the good green fertile smell of the higher layers.

I stop pitching. My fiancé looks at me and says, "What?"

I say, "You were already fucking her when she came and jumped in my pile of leaves." His chin drops toward his chest—down and slightly forward. He is hanging his head. I stare. Outside of poorly written fiction, I've never seen anyone actually do this.

"Fuck you," I say. I drop the pitchfork and walk away.

We jogged together a few times last fall, you and I and he, on crisp mornings before we had to teach. Once, we ran down a street littered with smooth, dark chestnuts and crimson maple leaves, and you stopped to pick some up. You were always picking up leaves that fall, always twirling one in your hand. You kept a crystal bowl of them on a credenza in your dining room, next to your elegant cut-glass decanter of whiskey. Everyone brought you pretty leaves. Even I saved a particularly striking or large or intact one for you to add to your collection.

Of course, my fiancé picked up chestnuts and leaves for you, too, on that run. He handed them to you the way a cat drops a dead mouse at the feet of its owner: I love you, here is a present.

I flung pillowcases up and up and they kept slipping down on my head. I wondered why I didn't just get a chair to stand on inside the linen closet. Then Jay was filling the doorframe, standing close behind me.

He said, "I have to tell you something."

I said, "Okay."

He said, "I did a very bad thing."

I sat down on the edge of the bed, and he sat beside me. I looked at the cracks in the cool green walls.

In October, you walked down our block as I raked the leaves. You and your husband had just moved into a house two blocks away, and the bus let you off a block from our house. The two of you came by often; you dropped in for drinks on our porch or impromptu bocce in our long backyard. Several mornings a week, we had breakfast at each other's house and drank coffee at dining room tables and graded papers. It was not improbable that you should come by now, although I do remember feeling mild surprise.

"Hello, friend," you said to me.

"Hello, friend," I replied. It was a charming habit you had, to call us friend, and it had caught on among all of us, we three couples who were close friends, practically inseparable. Jay and me, you and Daniel, Gil and Sarah. We called ourselves "the six," but some people called us the smug-marrieds, even though Jay and I were not yet married.

"Cute vest," you said. I thanked you but felt frumpy in it. That's why I wore it to rake the leaves.

Our front door was always open and my fiancé came out onto the porch.

"Hello, friend," he said.

"Hello, friend," you said to him.

You looked from him to me, back to him. Then you flopped backwards into the pile of leaves I'd raked onto the sidewalk.

I remember what you were wearing: a pink sweater, a pleated knee-length denim skirt, white go-go boots. You were carrying your white purse and leather teaching satchel. Splayed in the leaves, you looked like a Vogue model, and I told you so.

You didn't say anything, but you smiled at my fiancé, and he smiled at you. I smiled, too. We were all sharing a little joke I didn't understand.

In the days after he tells me but before we start installing the bamboo floors, I throw everything you ever gave to me or to him into the trashcan by the peony bushes.

Sage-green, scallop-edge ceramic bowls.

The brown cotton poncho you gave me the morning of my birthday.

The cape you sewed me to go with my superhero costume for that last Halloween party. I was Gatorade Girl.

A navy-and-white-striped headband you bought me at the dollar store, which you loved. You used to buy so much there. One day in February, after you had stopped sleeping with my fiancé and were already sleeping with Gil, we went to the dollar store together to buy balloons for a party. Impulsively, I bought paper lanterns for my September wedding. You helped me decide on colors: green and orange. Some pink. I hung a couple at the party, but they were cheaply made and broke within hours.

Steve Ross's *Happy Yoga* book. "It's good for worry," you said when you gave it to me last Christmas, during the affair. "My sister and I trade it back it forth and keep it on our night tables," you said. I wondered for a moment what worried you so, but I did not ask. Instead, I said, "How thoughtful of you." I was very anxious in those days; in a month, I would take my oral exams.

Mix CDs with your handwriting on them, especially the one I had never seen before. Songs: Come away with me. You're always on my mind. Our love is better than ice cream.

I confront Jay on the porch steps. He says he doesn't remember receiving the CD.

She certainly didn't give it to me, I say.

When I think Jay and I might do this nebulous thing called "working it out," I wonder how I'll ever learn to like the bathroom again—this bathroom in which they fucked. It was always my favorite room in the house. I loved its vaulted ceilings, the old-fashioned door and doorknob, the pale green walls, the modern Scandinavian fixtures. I call my friend Denise, who teaches elementary school in Berkeley—she helped smudge the principal's office to get rid of its bad energy. You'll need sage, she tells me.

Instead, I stand naked in front of the wide bathroom mirror and masturbate. I am hornier than ever in these days when my fiancé doesn't touch me but doesn't leave me either, because now there is no one for whom to leave me. My fiancé wants a woman who no longer wants him, who after sleeping with him slept with his friend. It's pretty funny, actually, when you think about it.

Three times I see you, three days in a row, a week after Jay comes up behind me in the linen closet. Once I am biking and you are walking your dog. Again, I am biking and you are walking your dog. A third time, Jay and I walk to Liberty Heights Fresh in the morning for organic milk and eggs. You are wearing brown shorts, a brown tank top without a bra. I am wearing the sweet-potato-colored linen pants I wore the day Jay and I got engaged. We hold hands and walk down the sidewalk. I laugh when I see you ahead of us. The dog strains at his leash, pulling you toward us. You are very tan. In a moment of panicky indecision, I let go of Jay's hand as he lets go of mine. We step onto the grass on either side of the sidewalk. I hate myself even as I do it, knowing I should force you around me.

"So, hi," you say, and you look as if you might cry.

"Good morning," I say, with a little singsong lilt because I am with my man and you are not, although you have been. Also, I am pretending not to be bothered that Jay and I have stepped apart to let you pass.

Jay's face is flat and closed. He looks at you but does not say anything.

We install the new bamboo floors. I lay boards and Jay follows close behind with the pneumatic nailer. I used to call my mother every night, but now I call her less and less. When I do call, I talk about the new floors. Sometimes she asks if I have a cold. I say, "Allergies." Our conversations are short. I can tell she has questions she won't ask.

I wonder if I will stay long enough to enjoy these new floors. Hour to hour, I alternate between something I think is forgiveness and something that feels like rage. The forgiveness comes from my own guilt, from what I would want for myself from a woman on whose porch I once laid an armful of lilies.

Once the boards are nailed down and the furniture is back in place, we drive to Yellowstone for the long Fourth of July weekend. We went to Yellowstone this time last year as well. I studied for my exams, and Jay cooked all our meals. Sometimes we packed books and lunches and beer and hiked to scenic spots. One morning we encountered a baby black bear by the Lamar River and tasted real fear. I read *The Five Books of Moses* in a captain's chair, and Jay joked that I was reading "Five Buck Mimosas." It was a magical time. We'd just moved in together. In slightly over a year, we'd get married in a small town in Southern Idaho.

On this drive to Yellowstone, a year later, Jay and I discuss whether or not one bad act undermines every kindness a person has performed. Jay says it doesn't, and I think it does.

In the fall, I practiced bus tonglen on the way to and from teaching. Tonglen was something I'd read about in a book on Eastern religions. I adapted it for my bus rides. I looked at each person on the bus and wished them well, wished them a good day. This practice was for my own anxiety about taking my exams. I could not read on the bus without feeling nauseous, and I did not own an iPod. There was nothing I could do on the bus but be alone with my own thoughts. Then I decided I could imagine each person's worries and wish them peace.

Now I think of myself riding the bus to campus, up 1700 South, then 1500 East, past Sunnyside-Guardsman, the Steiner Aquatic Center, and the Tennis Center. The entire time I wished peace for the concertina player, the professor who wears a top hat and black overcoat and looks like a penguin, the middle-aged mom with her pink-coated daughter. Back home, my fiancé and my friend fucked. Sometimes in my house, sometimes in hers.

On New Year's Eve, when everyone was back from visiting family, the six of us exchanged gifts and had raclette dinner at Jay's and my house. Then we opened our house to a wider circle of friends. There was cider and wine, and some friends brought guitars and played music on couches, and someone saw you bawling in the kitchen. I assume Jay had said why can't we just continue the way we are, having these secret meetings—she has to teach five days a week next semester instead of two, so we'll have that much more time. But that wasn't what you wanted.

You cried in my kitchen, and Jay held you in his arms. In another room, oblivious, I sat on a couch with friends and sang "Auld Lang Syne" and Christmas carols, although Christmas was already over.

Then you left the party. You said good night to me and I could see you'd been crying. I said are you okay, and you said, yes, this song just makes me sad. We were singing "Downtown," by Petula Clark. Daniel drove home, you in the passenger's seat, and later I found out that you would not get out of the car. You cried in the driveway for three hours. Daniel thought you were going crazy.

In February, after your affair with Jay had ended and you had begun your affair with Gil, I lent you my copy of Stegner's *Crossing to Safety*. For months, Jay had been lending you graphic novels to read, and I was jealous. I wanted you to read something of mine.

I held *Crossing to Safety* out to you in your living room, and I said, "It's so good. It's about these two academic couples and friendship. It reminds me of us. I think there's an affair in it. That part doesn't remind me of us. But anyway, it's just so beautiful, so sweet."

I remember the look on your face when I said, "I think there's an affair in it." I didn't know then what to make of that look.

You gave the book back to me a week later. You said, "It's such a simple story." It sounded condescending even then: as if you were saying I was a little simple. Which I was.

I re-read the book because I couldn't remember if there was an affair in it or not. There wasn't. Laughing, I said to Jay: "I told Emily that there was an affair in this book, but I was wrong. It was polio." He laughed, too.

Later, after Jay came up behind me in the linen closet, I fantasized about all the terrible things that could happen to you. Polio was one of them.

Yellowstone. Slough Creek. At the campsite, I ask Jay not to call me "friend." Good morning, friend, how are you friend. It's what

98

you used to say to her, too, I say. It's what she used to say to me, it's what all three of us called each other. The way you said it to her, what you meant by friend, was so different from the way you said it to me.

He calls me *compadre* instead. And still, for some reason, I think we might be able to work it out.

Last summer, when Jay was out of town at a comic book convention, you and Daniel and I went to a friend's wedding reception. It was late July, and in about a month, you would kiss my fiancé for the first time in a hotel room in Cedar City.

After the reception, we went to your house and drank whiskey. You still lived on Denver Street. You were wearing a pink striped seersucker dress, and you looked elegant and charming, as you always did. You sat on the couch with your bare legs stretched out in front of you on the cushions. Languid—that's how I remember you that night—and I remember thinking how pretty your tan legs were against the pink of your dress. I had never liked whiskey, but I liked it that night. I liked the weight of the glass tumblers, the soft light, and the music Daniel put on the stereo. I missed my fiancé, but I was okay, I was happy. I noticed your new IKEA coffee table, stark black, and on it, a dog-eared copy of *Anna Karenina*. I had never read it. I asked you about it. I don't remember what you said, but I remember your shrug, the slight lift and drop of your bare brown shoulders.

Once, I walked in on the two of you looking at a graphic novel in Jay's study. It was the November of your affair because the air mattress was still blown up from Denise's visit. The mattress was losing air and the two of you were creating a dip, falling into each other, your sides touching. I stood in the doorway and said in my singsong way: "Hey-guys." It was what I was always saying when I would finally hunt down the two of you in a dark corner of a bar or party. Your thighs would be touching; you'd be talking, laughing. Hey guys, I'd say. Hey guys, look at me. Hey guys, what about me.

***

When we camp, we always bring with us more books than we can read.

"Whoever reads more of the books they brought owes the other person something," I say.

Jay mixes canned beans and corn and bottled vinaigrette as salad to accompany dutch-oven enchiladas—his specialty.

"Okay," he says. "Like what?"

"Like a Space Burger and Tastee Treat on the way home."

"I was going to say fidelity," Jay says.

"Why don't we start with something manageable?" I say.

I am chopping the onions. That is always my job. They never make me cry.

A few weeks before my fiancé told me about you and him, but after you'd already been banished from our social scene for sleeping with Gil, you came by our house when we were not there and laid on the doormat a pink paper gift bag containing magenta peonies. (From my garden, you wrote in the note. They're going crazy, the peonies, you wrote.) The bag also held a pie pan we'd brought once to a dinner at your house, and a king-sized Reese's Peanut Butter Cup, Jay's favorite. He took it out of the bag and put it in the freezer. He likes them frozen. As you probably know.

Touched by your gesture, I sent you a note. Thank you for the peonies, I said. I hope you're doing well. We miss you.

A couple weeks later, another friend told me that peony buds won't open until ants crawl over them. A couple weeks after that, Jay stood behind me in the linen closet and said he'd done something bad. A couple weeks after that, the peonies in Jay's and my yard opened, and I couldn't wait for them to die.

One night in January, I initiated sex. Jay could not maintain an erection. He rolled off of me, and I rolled over onto my stomach. I propped myself up on my elbows and stared in the dark at where I thought his face was.

"Are you not attracted to me anymore?" I was scared but wanted to know.

"Of course I'm attracted to you," he said.

"Because if that's it," I said, "you can tell me. If you don't want to be with me, I'll be sad but it won't kill me."

"That's not it," he said. "Of course I want to be with you."

Jay had never not gotten an erection when I put the moves on him. Not even all fall, when he was having sex with you. But once you ended the affair with Jay to sleep with Gil, he got too depressed to get it up.

In Yellowstone, I read books on fidelity and how to save a marriage after an affair. There are no books on how to save an engagement, which makes me nervous. It implies there is no reason to save it; you should just get the hell out of dodge.

At the Lamar River, we find a little dock and set our captain's chairs on it. A red cooler full of beer sits between us. I read while Jay sketches the current.

My book says a marriage isn't doomed after an affair if the unfaithful partner learns from his mistakes.

"Do you think you can really learn from this?" I look over at him.

Jay says, "Of course." He does not look up from his sketch.

I say, "It's demeaning—to think of my pain as a learning opportunity for you. I don't think there is learning from this. There is only doing it again or not doing it again."

"So you don't think you learned anything from that married guy?"

"No," I say. "I don't think so."

"Well," he says. "That's sad."

It takes a few hours, but eventually, I boil inside.

When Jay recited his tinny, stilted phrases on the edge of the bed, I stared at the cracks and thought of the married man. When I was in college, a professor I had a crush on said he was in love with me. He was married and much older. I worked for him—spilling fruit flies out of cotton-plugged vials and sorting them according to sex. And then one night I gave in. I was graduating in a week, moving to a new city. It turned out that his wife was away. He said he just wanted to spend the night with me. He said he wanted only to hold me, that nothing more had to happen. He said it would be like camping. I pretended to believe him.

All June and July I have been looking in the mirror, pretending I am looking at you. Through hot angry screwed-up-face tears I whisper, "I hate you, I hate you, you whore."

Of course, I am also looking at myself.

When Jay finished telling me about the bad thing he'd done, I turned from the cracks in the wall and looked at him.

"I understand," I said. "I think I understand. Once I did something bad, too."

"You did?" he said. His face lit up with ecstatic hunger.

"I did," I said. "I told you once before. You listened but you didn't hear. I asked you the worst thing you'd ever done. You said you stood up a girl you were supposed to travel with in England. I didn't think that was so bad. Pretty bad, but not despicable. I told you the worst thing I'd ever done. I spent a night with a married man. We didn't have sex sex. But it doesn't matter. I've always felt guilty about it. So I understand how it can happen."

I will always believe you seduced Jay, even though I know he probably seduced you. He was always convincing people to do things, to come to a party, to come out for drinks when they needed to study or go to bed early to fight off a cold. "Sure, go ahead," he'd say. "Go home and rub Vagisil on your pussy."

Betrayal by a female friend may be even more piercing than betrayal by a man. I want to sleep with your new husband when you have one. I want to fuck him in your basement, in your bedroom, in

102

your bathroom up against the sink. I want to fuck him everywhere and then I want you to find us curled in sweat-soaked sheets.

But if your new husband is Gil, then I don't want to do any of that.

We are camping on the Fourth of July weekend. Nine years ago on the Fourth of July, the professor and I had gone to see the fireworks in the park. Afterward, he and I lay on blankets on the floor of my apartment; my friends had already hauled my mattress and bed frame and most of my furniture to my new city. So, in some ways, it was just like camping.

The married man went down on me, but I could not go down on him. "I'm sorry," I said. "I just can't."

We lay quietly for a while, and then I turned to him and said, "I feel like I just crossed a line I hope no one ever crosses with me."

He said, "Mmm-hmm."

I lay there wondering how I would feel in ten years. I still haven't been able to toss the little stuffed koala he gave me as a graduation present. I wonder if I unconsciously chose Jay precisely to punish me for that crime.

About two months ago, in May, when I knew of your affair with Gil but not with Jay, we ran into you at the symphony. I felt frumpy and you wore a purple dress with a little yellow shrug and purple pumps. You were still wearing your wedding ring even though we all knew you didn't want to be married.

Jay and his mother and I walked across the plaza at Abravanel Hall; you walked slightly ahead of us. Jay caught up with you and you turned around. You seemed surprised, guarded, pleasant. You said you were on a date with yourself.

We walked into the lobby together, but we got separated from you. Jay said he was going to go find you, try to talk to you. Of course, I said. We hadn't seen you since the affair with Gil had come out. We missed you. Well, I missed you. Jay had seen you more times than I knew. He had gone to coffee at Coachman's with you, yes, but he was also coming round your house, begging you to dump Gil, begging you to take him back.

I waited with Jay's mother.

"So that's her," she said. We'd told Jay's parents that our four closest friends were splitting up because of an affair. Tragic, we said. So sad.

"She's a lovely girl, isn't she?" my future mother-in-law said.

"Yes," I said. "She is."

In Lava Hot Springs, in December, when you and Jay had been sleeping together for almost four months, I came into your hotel room and saw your panties bunched in the jeans you stepped out of to change into your bathing suit. I noticed they were gray and all lace. Seeing them felt intimate, transgressive.

Last fall when we moved you into your new house, Jay carried in a dresser drawer full of clothes. He set it down on the bare mattress, took out a pair of your panties, and shot them like a rubber band across the room. You blushed and retrieved them, and you and he exchanged glances, smiles, although yours was more nervous— your husband was there, after all, and so was I. Maybe those were the panties Jay had peeled off your body with his teeth, and now he was flinging them over your head for everyone to see. The reminder of what the two of you had done was in plain sight but meant nothing to me, dutifully, cheerfully, carrying your heavy boxes.

The morning after I heard of your affair with Gil, you called me. You said you had a threatening student. He'd made some weird comments over email, and now he was coming to your cubicle for office hours, and you wondered if I would just sit in a cubicle nearby in case something happened.

I went to your cubicle immediately. You were there. The student had already come. It was fine, you said. You needn't have worried, you said. You were sorry to bother me. Thank you for coming.

I got ready to leave. But I had to say something. I knelt by your chair. Sarah told me, I said. I know, you said. You started to cry. I reached for your hand and you grasped mine.

I smoothed your hair and kissed the top of your head.

And then I said, "I've been you, I've been Gil, I know what it's like to have guilt." You looked at me sharply. I felt I'd touched you, lightened your load somehow. "I know how hard it is to forgive yourself," I said. I was thinking that I've been you, I've been Gil, but I've never been Sarah.

That same day, I went to the library and brought home a stack of books on affair-proofing your marriage. When I came in the house, Jay sat hunched over his laptop at the dining room table. I showed him the titles. One of them was *How to Make Love to the Same Person for the Rest of Your Life*. I was shy, embarrassed, hopeful.

"I want us to make it," I said.

"Me, too," he said.

Last summer, the six of us camped at Alta exactly one week before we all went to Cedar City and you began your affair. In Alta, you wore tank tops without a bra so we could all see your tiny breasts and hard nipples. Sarah, intuiting a threat that I had not, gave you silicone nipple shields for your birthday the week before, but you did not wear them.

At night, you and Jay lay in the road to look at stars, and, of course, I lay with you. Jay was my fiancé—why shouldn't I be there? I thought I was letting you share in our romantic moment, and it turns out I was sharing in yours.

I can't help thinking about this tonight in Yellowstone, because Jay and I are camping, and there is a crescent moon and a sky full of stars, and it isn't romantic, not one bit.

In March, you fucked Gil on Sarah's thirtieth birthday. She had gone out of town with a friend. Gil didn't go with her. He had said he needed some space. They were in counseling, although Gil had not yet admitted to the affair. You and Jay and I were supposed to go for a long run together, so I emailed you to ask what time. You said you seemed to be getting a cold, that you had "the sniffles."

When Jay and I went to the grocery store, I bought you flowers. We walked them over to your house.

"You're a nice person," Jay said as we walked.

"No, I'm not," I said. "Emily's just always been sweet to me."

We took over the flowers, and I remember Jay standing a step behind me, hands thrust deep in his coat pockets. It was cold. His face was closed. He knew about Gil, knew exactly what was happening that weekend. Gil might even have been there, in the house. Daniel was in Seattle, visiting his brother.

You, Emily, looked sallow. You wore a little purple chiffon scarf around your neck. I loved and admired the way you wore your scarves—all last fall when you wore your butter yellow scarf carefully folded and tied jauntily around your neck. For a while, I searched for a scarf that I could wear the same way. How beautiful I thought you were then.

In the middle of the night, I awake in the tent. I think I hear a bear. The ranger told us one came through on June 27. I can't sleep for other reasons, too. Jay nestles in his sleeping bag beside me. He seems to sleep peacefully.

It's done, I decide in the middle of the night. It's not that he's scared of marriage, or monogamy. He didn't like having sex with me and he likes having sex with her. I won't spend the rest of my life trying to convince him I'm worthy. Enough prancing around in new underwear in the mornings, hoping he'll notice.

For the rest of the night, I stare at the ceiling of the tent in the darkness. At the first gray hint of light, I unzip my bag and drag a captain's chair to the stream. I shiver at its edge until dawn. Then I stand up and make the coffee.

In the car on the drive home, I call my mother. I have not called her in weeks. She won't call me, but she worries. I tell her about all the things Jay cooked in the dutch oven.

"You lucky," she says.

I ask her what she had for dinner.

✳✳✳

Something breaks in me during that long night in the tent, but still I am not ready to leave. A week after we return from Yellowstone, we go to Liberty Park to discuss postponing our wedding—only postponing it, not calling it off. We sit on a bench, and I ask him if he fondled her in the hot springs, where the six of us were naked and the freight train cut by on the mountain and lit up the pool and made leaf shadows in the steam, and through the lit steam I could see the spot under the oak where we'd say our vows and where I would hang paper lanterns.

He says, yes, they'd fondled each other under the water, while I swam and waded and laughed a few feet away, and gazed onto the lawn with the oak tree. His penis against her brown thighs. Her fingers splayed and buried in the reddish hair above his ass. All under the cover of water and steam.

"You're sick," I say.

"I know," he says and begins to cry.

"You deserve each other, you fuckers," I say. "Fuck you. Fuck fuck fuck all of you."

After postponing the wedding, we visit the couples counselor one more time. She tells us to try having sex again. Relax, she says. Have a glass of wine.

That night Jay comes to me in the bathroom while I floss. He stands in the doorway.

"I guess we should try it," he says. He shuffles away in his old-man slippers. He looks as if I've just asked him to clean the rain gutters.

He downloads French porn and waits for me in bed with the laptop on the mattress. We have sex while he watches it. It is the last time.

Over Sunday brunch in late July, a friend tells me about two other women. We both know it is a matter of "at least" two, but neither of us says so. She says it is not her place to say who the women are. She says only that they have told her, and she thinks they should tell me. That if they will not, she will.

I go home. I ask Jay. He says he does not know what the friend is talking about. I ask if he's saying it didn't happen. He says, no, I'm sure it probably did. I just don't remember. He calls the friend. She tells him who, when. He remembers.

In the kitchen, I sink down to the slate green tiles of the floor. I am laughing. I lean my head against the kitchen island. The night after he came up behind me in the linen closet, I spent an entire evening scrubbing the grout of this floor with a toothbrush. It took me three hours. I sipped from a glass of whiskey the whole time.

I am packing to move out. I find the small toy koala the professor gave me before I moved to Utah. I put it in a box and include a note. I explain that my fiancé has had an affair and we are splitting up. I do not feel right keeping the koala anymore. He writes back that he fell in love with me when he needed to get through a difficult period. He and his wife are happy now; I never hurt her.

But this is what he does not understand: It is possible to hurt without knowing you hurt. I hurt for months—*hey guys, what about me?* Pain isn't contingent on knowledge. The knowledge is, in fact, the beginning of the end of the pain.

I go home for a week before I return to find an apartment. At my mother's kitchen table, I tell her what has happened, why there will be no wedding. She puts her elbows on the table and covers her face with her hands. Then she looks up and leans across the table. She smoothes my hair, then tucks it behind my ear.

"I always liked when you put your hair back behind your ears," she says. "I could see your pretty face. Oh, my child," she says. "My little star."

Then she straightens, looks at me, and says, "You know it is not worst thing."

"You're right," I say. "It's not."

She stands up, crosses the kitchen. At the sink, she turns on the water to fill the basin full of dirty dishes. She presses a palm to her lower back.

"It's good you left," she says.

108

***

Jay hated dreams in fiction. They're so overdetermined, he said.

Indeed: I am in a Central American nation, in some kind of tile-floored refugee compound with many other people. A grid has been drawn on the ground, and each of us lies face down in one cell of the grid. A gunman steps among our bodies and shoots us. When he gets to me, he shoots me in the back of the head several times. I see my blood everywhere. I feel the impact of the gunshots but no pain, only fear. The gunman steps away and shoots someone else. I know I must not be dead because I have an awareness that he is coming around to shoot me again. He does.

I wake from my own death. I begin to name it.

About the Author

Halina Duraj's stories have appeared in *The Sun*, *The Harvard Review*, *Fiction*, *Witness*, and other journals. She has an MA in creative writing from the University of California, Davis, and a PhD in literature and creative writing from the University of Utah. In 2012, she was a writer-in-residence at Hedgebrook, a women's writing retreat on Whidbey Island, WA. She teaches at the University of San Diego, where she also directs the Lindsay J. Cropper Center for Creative Writing.